Desire & Deceit

A Victorian Crime Thriller

Carol Hedges

Little G Books

For My Family

About the Author

Carol Hedges is the successful British author of 19 books for teenagers and adults. Her writing has received much critical acclaim, and her novel Jigsaw was shortlisted for the Angus Book Award and longlisted for the Carnegie Medal.

Carol was born in Hertfordshire, and after university, where she gained a BA (Hons.) in English Literature & Archaeology, she trained as a children's librarian. She worked for the London Borough of Camden for many years subsequently re-training as a secondary school teacher when her daughter was born.

The Victorian Detectives series

Diamonds & Dust
Honour & Obey
Death & Dominion
Rack & Ruin
Wonders & Wickedness
Fear & Phantoms
Intrigue & Infamy
Fame & Fortune

Acknowledgments

Many thanks to Gina Dickerson, of RoseWolf Design, for another superb cover, and to my editor.

I also acknowledge my debt to all those amazing Victorian novelists for lighting the path through the fog with their genius. Unworthily, but optimistically, I follow in their footsteps.

Desire & Deceit

A Victorian Crime Thriller

'The end is where we start from.' ~ *T. S. Eliot*

London, 1868. It is June, and predicted to be the hottest summer on record, they say. Day after day of clear blue skies. The sun beats down. Flaming June. Trees in the great parks droop, the swans on the river are stunned. The city swelters and suffers in the unforgiving heat. London was not made for this: it was built for rain ~ its grey stone buildings suit short days and cold nights.

Now, the streets run with melted tar and smell of equine by-products, and carts go around in the early morning spraying water to set the dust that billows up in choking clouds. The population wilt, sweat and itch in their heavy clothing. Tempers are short; arguments flare over the smallest things: a seat on the underground, a perceived push on a white-hot pavement, the last jam tart in a baker's shop.

The cheese trade suffers badly. Labourers in the agricultural industry suffer fatally. A man is found dead in a field of peas that he'd been gathering. But, even in the sweltering unbearable heat, some find beauty as the eternal mists around St Paul's turn to a glittering haze and the darkest alleys flash golden glimpses in the spendthrift of sunshine.

Sadly, this golden state does not exist here, in the building that houses Scotland Yard's famous (or infamous, depending upon which side your crime is committed) detective division. Take Detective Inspector Leo Stride, for instance, who is missing his mugs of treacly black coffee, as the usual coffee-stall holders have betaken themselves to the countryside to escape the London inferno.

Stride's caffeine deficiency is manifesting itself in a growing reluctance to tolerate the sloppy written reports that land on his desk every morning from the night patrols, which are now being read with an even more rigid adherence to the correct use of the comma, the apostrophe and the spelling of 'criminal intent'. He is just engaged in a vicious red-pencilling attack on the latest one, when he is interrupted by his colleague, Detective Sergeant Jack Cully.

"Message from Robertson: he wishes to see us urgently," he says.

Stride raises his head wearily. "Why?"

Jack Cully gives a 'search-me' shrug.

"Right then," Stride says grimly, hauling himself to his feet, "let us not keep the good surgeon waiting."

The two detectives cross the yard and descend the steps that lead to the police morgue, a cool, white-washed set of rooms, where the various victims of crime are brought to be forensically studied and dissected. Here, Robertson, the dour police surgeon, assisted by his latest medical student, reigns supreme. His disdain for the intellectual abilities and medical knowledge of members of the police force is legendary. His acerbic remarks cut as sharply as the various knives of his trade. He and Stride spar regularly. Stride rarely wins.

Entering the morgue, Stride feels the temperature drop. Compared to the searing heat outside, the room is pleasantly cool. If it wasn't for the occupants, alive and dead, coupled with the smell of chemicals, it would be a fine place to work during the unbearable heatwave gripping the city.

Robertson steps out from behind the wooden dissecting table. "Ah. Here you both are. Thank you for your prompt attendance. A problem has occurred, to which I felt I should draw your attention. It concerns a body."

Stride glances at the table. "I see no body."

Robertson fixes him with a glittering eye. "Indeed, you do not, detective inspector. Your powers of observation are, as always, beyond reproach. The point is, you should see a body. There was a body brought here in the early hours of the morning. I was informed of its presence when I arrived, and came straight here, intending to commence my examination first thing."

"So where is it now?"

Robertson shakes his head and makes a palms-up gesture. "That is what I also wish to know, and why I sent for you post-haste."

"You are seriously telling us that someone stole a dead body?" Cully asks.

"Unlikely as it may appear, that would seem to be the case," Robertson replies drily. "*Nos non habemus corpus* as it were. I am sure I do not need to provide a translation. And I would hardly tell you such information frivolously, detective sergeant."

Stride sucks in his breath. "But how did they get it past the desk constable?"

In response, Robertson leads the way through to the small storeroom at the back, in which the various chemicals, enamel dishes and tools of the trade are kept, stacked neatly on shelves or locked in a glass cabinet.

"It appears that initial access was gained via breaking a pane in the window over the sink. Once achieved, the door was opened and the body removed."

The two detectives examine the broken window pane thoroughly. Then turn their attention to the door.

"Why isn't there a better lock on this door?" Stride asks. "It's only fastened by a single bolt."

"Over the years it was thought hardly necessary to secure it; after all, it's not as if anyone is going to try to escape."

Cully opens the door and peers out. "It seems to lead to a small alley."

"That is correct. It is the way the constables deliver the bodies. It was thought that to see them brought in by the main entrance might cause alarm to the ladies and those of a delicate disposition. The alley leads to a small side-street with high walls on each side. It is unlikely that anyone would have blundered in accidentally."

"Who would want to steal a dead body?" Stride muses.

"Your question is most apposite," Robertson replies. "Who indeed? Especially given the current inclement weather."

"Do you think it was taken for medical reasons?" Cully asks.

"Ah, detective sergeant, that is indeed a possibility I have considered myself. Therefore, I have taken the liberty of dispatching young Mr Bennet to make inquiries of local teaching hospitals ~ I decided that he, being of the medical fraternity and also newly qualified, might arouse less suspicion than your good selves."

"Very wise," Stride grunts.

Robertson makes him a small mock bow. "Your approbation of my sagacity is much appreciated, detective inspector," he says drily. He eyes Stride speculatively. "I also assumed, given the ungodly times we inhabit, that this was not a case of *furta sacra*. Do you not agree?"

"Can you tell us anything about the dead individual?" Cully inquires quickly, before Stride can chip in with a sarcastic comment or Robertson launch into one of his lengthy explanations of holy relics stolen throughout the centuries.

Robertson shakes his head. "I know as much as you do. I expect that the constable who brought him in has left a report on one of your desks. No doubt that will fill in the necessary details that I am, alas, unable to supply. I confess I was looking forward to dissecting something. Since the heatwave arrived, there haven't been many corpses brought in."

4

Stride nods. "Ah. Yes. I hadn't got around to reading the latest reports," he says. "I'll do it right away." He prepares to leave the mortuary.

"Festina lente," Robertson calls after him. "It is much too hot to hurry."

The detectives make their way back to Stride's office. Even at this hour, the air is thick and gravid and both men are sweating by the time they collapse into two chairs. Stride skims through a couple of reports, eventually extracting one. "Here it is. Night Constable Tom Williams. Now then, what does he have to say?"

Stride runs his gaze down the sheet of paper, occasionally murmuring "Uh-huh," as he does so. He looks up.

"Remarkable. How refreshing to read a report that doesn't begin every paragraph with 'I was proceeding,'" he says. "Young Constable Williams has clearly had some sort of reasonable education. He can punctuate. More remarkably, he has mastered the use of the apostrophe. Is he still around, do you suppose? I should like to question him about certain aspects of his report."

Cully goes to find out, returning sometime later accompanied by a rather sleepy young officer, who'd been attempting to snatch a quick nap in one of the police dormitories where the newest recruits live.

"This is Constable Williams," he says, waving the constable to the chair he'd recently vacated. Cully moves to stand next to Stride, behind the desk. He studies the young man. He is of regulation height, well-built. He has dark eyes, brown hair and a frank, open countenance. He regards his two superiors steadily as he waits to be enlightened as to why he has been summoned.

"The constable was telling me that it was his first turn on night duty," Cully says to Stride.

"I see," Stride says, nodding. "And your first dead body?"

The young man pulls a face and nods. "Yes, sir. It was."

"Well, it certainly won't be your last," Stride tells him. He picks up the piece of paper. "Now, about your report ..."

"Is there something amiss with my report, sir?" the constable asks, glancing from one man to the other.

Both Stride and Cully mentally note the use of 'amiss', not a word associated usually with the vocabulary of the lower ranks of the Metropolitan Police.

"The report is fine," Stride reassures him. "Very clear and well written. You discovered a young man, lying dead. You examined him. You noted that the body was still warm and rigor mortis had not set in. You also noted he was lying on his side, curled up in a strange way, and that the expression upon his face was such that you decided, on these bases, the man should be taken to the police mortuary, as you did not like to leave him where you found him.

"The problem is that he appears to have gone missing. So, I just wanted to go through the events of last night with you once more, to see if you might recall anything that could help us understand why somebody should break into the mortuary to remove a dead body.

"You have given me the facts, now let us see if you can give me your impressions. What do you remember about the body itself, and what made you decide to transfer it to the mortuary rather than just notifying the authorities of its presence?"

Constable Williams wrinkles his forehead and clasps his hands together as he bends his mind to focus upon events that have already been and gone. The two detectives watch his cogitations in silence. It is a technique honed from years of interrogation. (In their time, they have, between them, outwaited some of the most criminal elements of the city.)

"I thought it strange that a man so well dressed should be found dead in such an obscure location," he says. "I made a quick search of his person, and his watch, rings and other personal items were in place, so he had not been robbed. But something about his presence in the particular place and the way he was lying, set alarm bells ringing in my mind. The spot is right by a building site and is not near any places of entertainment or public houses. I saw no logical reason for him being there. So, I decided to err on the side of caution, as it were, and send for the night wagon."

"Thank you. That is very well observed," Stride says, nodding. "You may go now, constable. You have done your duty and done it well."

The young man's face lights up with a smile. "I thank you, sir." He rises and leaves the room.

"Constable Williams is clearly a young man with an observant eye. We shall watch his progress with interest," Stride remarks.

Scarcely has the door closed upon Scotland Yard's newest recruit, when a brief note is brought in from Robertson. His assistant has returned, having made discreet inquiries of various medical establishments. As term ended some time ago, there is no need for any corpses as there are no anatomy students to dissect them. Therefore, as far as he is concerned, Robertson has nothing further to contribute. There is no body to work upon. The note ends with a scrawled signature and a reference to someone called Asclepius, that Stride doesn't understand.

"Ah well, that is that," Stride says. "I had hoped the man would turn up on some dissecting table and give us something to investigate."

"But we have a break in, and the theft of a dead body," Cully says. "Surely that should be investigated?"

Stride spreads his hands in a gesture of defeat, "Is there any point? The body has gone; we are none the wiser as to who he was and why he was taken, and we probably never will be."

Sadly, like many of his predictions, events are once again going to prove Detective Inspector Stride completely wrong.

****

In the past ~ and by 'past' we mean the early part of the century, to travel from Bristol to London would have been a journey of over two days, jolting along rutted roads in a bone-shaking coach, stopping at wayside inns where the food might be execrable and the beds damp.

But now there is the miracle of the railway, and a journey only previously undertaken in dire necessity can be completed in comfort and in a coach pulled by an engine, not by four horses. And so here they are, the Harbinger family: father, mother, ten-year-old twins Hanover and Harriet, baby Timothy, their luggage and a small parrot in a cage. Bags, baggage and beings, they take up a whole second-class carriage.

The reason for their journey is simple. Aunt Euphemia Harbinger is dying. Finally. And when an aged family member is preparing their soul to cross that river into the unknown realm beyond, it is important that the family gathers round them. Especially when the aforementioned family member lives in a nice house in Chelsea and is the possessor of jewels, pictures and allegedly, a great deal of money.

Then, it is even more important to be at their bedside, letting their fading gaze dwell upon the innocent faces of their beloved nephew and his children, so that any thoughts in the way of the bequeathing of worldly goods and chattels should be made as easy as possible for them.

So here they are. The Great Western Railway locomotive chugs through parched fields and tinder-dry woodland. Occasionally it sweeps through small stations, where people stand in glazed immobility to watch it pass. The family sweat and fidget. The baby whimpers uncomfortably. The parrot sulks under its green baize cover.

"Now then," the *paterfamilias* reminds them, "when we reach London, we will take a cab straight to our hotel, where we will change into our best clothes before going to see your great aunt."

"But Papa, shouldn't we change into our worst clothes, as we want her to think we are very poor, so she gives us all her money?" asks Harriet, who has been described by various ex-governesses as little Miss Knowitall, and not in a favourable way.

Her father frowns and pulls at his moustache. She is a puzzle, this girl. A conundrum, a riddle, an enigma. Everything about her is sharp: the cutting attitude of her eyes, the edge of her mouth, her blade-like face. Even her dark hair falls from her head like a million sharp spears. Far too clever and far too inclined to speak her mind. He shudders to think what she will be like when she grows up. If the previous couple of years are any indication, she will be on his hands for the rest of her life.

"We will do exactly as I have instructed," he says sternly. "Indeed, thinking about it, I believe you and Mama should remain at the hotel. After all, it is mainly for Hanover and his future that we are here. And, in time, Timothy of course. Rugby, Oxford and the Law do not come cheap."

His daughter shoots him a sharp look out of lidded grey eyes that are far too knowing for a person of her age. "Will Uncle Arthur and Aunt Wilhelmina be there?" she asks, innocence hanging like loops of toffee from her words.

He winces. There is the nub of the problem. The reason for the hasty departure. The three siblings have always, throughout their lives, competed with each other for everything. And he, as the second son, has had to compete the hardest, has had the most to lose. An heir and a spare. Always. From the last sweet in the bag to the apportioning of their dead parents' estate, he has been bested by his older brother at every turn. There is no measure for the sense of grievance Sherborne Harbinger has carried round all his adult life.

"I expect they will be present," he says, gritting his teeth. "After all, they are also family."

His daughter gives him a meaningful smile and is about to open her mouth to respond when her mama places a gloved hand warningly upon her knee.

"Your father has spoken, dear," she murmurs. "We will do exactly what he says. Now, would you like a biscuit? We are still some way away from London."

A bag of dry-looking biscuits is produced and shared round. Harriet takes one. Hanover smirks at his sister as he helps himself to three. Harriet nibbles at the unappetising snack, then feeds it furtively to the parrot. There is a universal belief that, due to their proximity in the womb, twins are born with some deep mystical connection that binds them together. The Harbinger twins are living evidence that one should never trust in universal beliefs.

The train finally huffs into Paddington Station. The family clamber out of the carriage. A porter is hailed. Luggage is stacked onto a trolley. The parrot complains loudly throughout the proceedings. They make their way to the barrier. The steam from the engines makes it like walking into a furnace. Outside the station, Sherborne

Harbinger hails a cab and bundles them all inside. The cases are distributed round and on the roof of the cab. The parrot is placed next to Harriet. It continues to squawk. They set off for their hotel. The cab horse stumbles along at a slower than walking pace, blowing out its nostrils in protest at having to pull a heavy load through the sun-baked streets.

At the Excelsior Hotel, the family de-cab and are shown to their suite of rooms by a tired-looking chamber maid in a limp cap. Father and son then change into crumpled suits and shirts, then set off to express their sympathy in person. The parrot goes with them. It has an important role. Arriving at the Chelsea house, Harbinger knocks in an imperious manner. The door is opened by Rose, the housekeeper, who regards them with some suspicion.

"I am afraid we do not entertain tinkers," she says. She shoots a glance at the parrot. "Nor buy from itinerant peddlers," she adds.

Sherborne sucks in an indignant breath and draws himself up to his full height. "I am Mr Sherborne Harbinger, the nephew of your mistress. Please announce us at once."

The housemaid pinches her lips and stands aside to let them enter. "My mistress is resting in her room. It is on the first floor, if you would care to follow me," she says.

They make their way up to the first floor, their footsteps muffled by the thick ruby-red carpet. They follow the housekeeper's ram-rod straight back along a silent corridor until she stops outside a closed door. The air smells of medicine and elderly body. Hanover wrinkles his nose. His father shoots him an admonishing glance.

"Now, Hanover, wipe that expression off your face. Remember why we are here. Make your bow and let your great aunt see that you are a gentleman."

"Hanover is a gentleman!" comes from under the green baize cloth.

"That's quite right, Polly. Be sure you tell Aunt Euphemia all about him. Just as we taught you."

The housekeeper knocks at the door. She signals to them to wait on the landing while she ascertains her mistress' wishes. After a few minutes, she returns.

"You may go in," she says, reluctantly.

Harbinger père et fils enter a room papered fearfully in blue roses and yellow lilies. The carpet is a dreary flat sandy-yellow in colour, as if the Sahara Desert had relocated to London. Swathed in a paisley shawl, Aunt Euphemia sits upright, propped against three pillows, in a four-poster bed draped in chintz hangings. She is wearing an old-fashioned lace cap with lappets. She regards her nephew and great nephew with an air of resigned weariness.

"Well, Sherborne, so here you are. And I see you have brought your son, young … young …" the old lady frowns.

"Hanover, dear aunt. His name is Hanover and he, as I, are sorry to see you so ill-disposed."

"I am not 'ill-disposed', Sherborne, I am dying. Were it not so, I doubt that you, and Arthur would have broken off from your various important lives to come and visit me, eh?" she snaps. "And what the devil is that thing the child holds in his hand?"

"Ah, dearest aunt, this is Polly ~ a young grey parrot. She is a present from my wife, my son Hanover and myself," Harbinger says. "We thought that her merry antics might amuse you. Hanover ~ take the cover off the cage and set it up over there ~ on the chest of drawers."

The old woman stares at the gift in horror. "And how am I supposed to look after this bird?"

"Oh, we have brought a bag of seeds. Your servant can fill the container and change the water. That is all the bird requires. Hanover will visit regularly to make sure she is looking after the parrot properly. I am sure you will find Polly a delightful companion."

The old woman's expression indicates she deeply and sincerely doubts it.

"And now, dear aunt, we will take our leave. We have only just arrived in London ~ we haven't even unpacked our cases; such was our eagerness to come to visit you. Till tomorrow ~ Hanover, make your bow to your dear great aunt."

The old woman waves a languid hand in dismissal, her eyes still fixed in horror on the parrot, who is turning somersaults on its perch and uttering strange squawking sounds. As soon as the housekeeper returns, she orders her to: "Take that disgusting bird away, Rose, and put it somewhere I shall not have to see or hear it again."

The housemaid picks up the cage.

"Go to your room, you ugly fright!" shrieks the parrot as it is unceremoniously bundled out. Then, *"Where is Harriet? I want Harriet!"*

****

Detective Sergeant Jack Cully has spent several hours painstakingly going through the various beat constable reports that somehow always end up on his desk instead of Detective Inspector Stride's. But as he scratches his head over the scrawly writing and spellings that some officer has taken a run at and missed, his mind keeps drifting back to the empty slab in the police mortuary, and the body that wasn't on it. Cully likes ends that are neatly tied and do not dangle precariously over some unfathomable edge.

Eventually, he decides to go and seek out Constable Tom Williams, and take the young officer and his own thoughts for a walk to where the body was first discovered, because a lot can be learned from observing a body *in situ*. Or in this case, the *situ*. Cully tries to approach every investigation with an absolutely blank mind, if possible. He prefers to observe first, and then draw inferences from his observations.

After a brief struggle through the pavement traffic, they arrive at a wooden hoarding, behind which the sound of loud rhythmic demolition hammers the air. A sign affixed to the hoarding informs the casual passer-by that the site has been acquired by Wm. Boxworth & Co. Developers. No Admittance Except by Appointment.

"I've been patrolling this beat regularly for a few weeks, sir," Constable Williams says. "When I started, it was just a row of ordinary houses. Older properties. Rented mainly. Irish navvies and elderly couples. Then they started digging up the pavement to make way for a railway line. A week ago, the hoarding went up and the houses started coming down. Now all the people have gone."

Cully knows it is a scene that repeats throughout the city and has done ever since he can remember. London is recreating itself, like some archaeological excavation in reverse. The past is being covered up and rewritten. The skyline changes constantly, spectral lines of half-demolished buildings, their rooms gaping like open wounds as the monstrous tentacles of the new city reach out to choke off the old one.

"Show me exactly where you found the body."

Constable Williams walks a short distance to where there is a gap in the hoarding. "He was lying here, sir. I saw his boots sticking out first. I thought he might be a drunk. Then, as I got closer, I realised he wasn't."

Jack Cully stands in silence, observing and thinking. Then he gets out his notebook and starts writing. He steps into the gap. On the other side of the hoarding, the ground falls steeply away into a deep trench. On a dark night, it would have been all too easy to trip, or be pushed over the edge, he thinks. The words 'lucky escape' do not seem relevant, given the circumstances.

Cully suddenly sees something glinting on the dusty ground at the base of the hoarding. He bends down and picks up a half-smoked cigar, its gold band intact. A further investigation elicits a wax vesta, half burned and coated with mud.

"See here?" he says. "What does this suggest?"

Constable Williams bites his lower lip. "It suggests maybe I didn't make a thorough enough search, sir."

Cully smiles. "It was dark, constable. Not your fault. Now, I'm not an expert on fine cigars, but from the name on the band, I don't think it was a cheap smoke. So, whose cigar was it? Our dead man's last smoke, or did it belong to someone associated with him? Does this suggest somebody else was present?" Cully pockets the cigar butt, and his notebook. "I wonder. Do you know the first rule of good detection, constable?" he continues. "Always ask yourself why. Why. Why did this happen? And keep on asking it, until you have the answer."

"Yes, sir. So why do you think somebody took the body out of the mortuary?"

"Indeed, that is the exact question that I am asking myself," Cully nods. "But I don't think we are going to find the answer here. Let us head back to Scotland Yard and plan the next move in our investigation."

****

The scene changes from a noisy building site to the far more salubrious environs of the Belvedere Club, off Pall Mall. In the magnificent high-ceilinged smoking-room we find Thomas Langland, Everard Carstairs and Arthur Harbinger. Butcher, baker, candlestick-maker. In reality, an MP, an entrepreneur and the senior manager of a large insurance company.

A substantial club luncheon of beef, batter pudding, gravy and potato, followed by jam roly-poly and custard sauce (the link between the menu of top London clubs and top public schools is never disputed) has been consumed, and is now being allowed to settle.

Waistcoat buttons have been undone. Well-fed bodies lounge deep in the comfortable leather armchairs. Pipes have been filled. Cigars cut and lit. Brandy in cut-crystal glasses are to hand. The atmosphere is heavy with repletion and smoke. The only sound is the rustle of newspapers and the odd gentle snore.

"So, Arthur," drawls Carstairs, entrepreneur, "how's that aunt of yours coming along. Seems to be takin' an unconscionable time about dying, eh!"

"It cannot be much longer now," Harbinger says, between gritted teeth.

"Better hadn't. You know the deal. Money up front by the end of the month or we shall have to bring old Bunter Faversham on board. Can't run a racing syndicate on promises of jam tomorrow. Need the chink to keep the wheels oiled."

Thomas Langland, MP, raises a quizzical eyebrow. "Want me to take soundings in the House? I'm sitting on the *Round up the Homeless and Put them to Useful Employment Committee* this afternoon. Faversham's chairing. I'm sure he'd fancy a slice of the pie."

"That won't be necessary," Harbinger says smoothly. "I shall be visiting my aunt in the next few days. I am sure there will be a positive outcome very shortly."

"Haw Haw! Going to put a pillow over the old gal's face yourself, are you?" Carstairs guffaws. "Like your style, Harbinger."

Arthur Harbinger bites his lower lip. Carstairs' words, though spoken in jest, have touched a nerve. Many a night he has lain awake, mulling over possible ways to hasten the dispatch of the old lady. And now his snaky younger brother and the brood of vipers have arrived, just to exacerbate the situation.

"Everything is in hand, don't fret. No need to call upon Faversham," he says.

Carstairs gives him a lowered eyebrow stare. "Glad to hear it, old man. Opportunities like this don't grow on trees. So, you'll be good for a couple of hundred, then?"

"Oh indeed, do not worry on that score" Harbinger says, rising to his feet and signalling to the waiter to fetch his coat, hat and stick. He descends the ornate staircase, then hurries out of the Belvedere and sets off down the street at a brisk pace. He is a man of business and right now, he has an important business appointment.

There is a world beneath the visible one, and some people have a different life to the one that they outwardly present. Such a person is Arthur Harbinger, a pale man with lank hair and cadaverous features. A man who conveys the impression of inhabiting some dark sulphurous nether region.

Harbinger was brought up in a bleak suburban household, with a father whose violent and unpredictable rages sent him and his younger brother and sister scurrying for sanctuary, and a mother who wore a veil indoors to hide her bruises and, when he was thirteen and away at boarding school, mysteriously disappeared, never to be mentioned again.

Left with three children, Harbinger's papa decided that a spare upbringing was the best way to bring them up and prepare them for the world that awaited. Food and praise were doled out sparingly. The only thing that was not spared was the rod.

The three motherless children were encouraged to compete for their father's attention, which, like the rest of their upbringing, was meted out in miniscule amounts and usually only to the one who could cite some sort of achievement. Preferably got at the expense of somebody else.

Cheating, lying, doing down an opponent, depriving a competitor of a prize ~ this was how the boys learned to win their father's notice and praise. Thus, Arthur became adept at copying the work of brighter schoolfellows and passing it off as his own, whilst Sherborne elevated tale-telling on his siblings and the servants into an art form. Growing out of childhood, the pinnacle of the paternal praise pyramid was the acquisition of money. The more, the better.

As for Wilhelmina, who was undereducated, disregarded and overlooked on account of being a girl, she spent a great deal of time in her room, singing to herself and plotting. Nobody was sure exactly what about. Nobody really cared.

Now, Arthur Harbinger crosses the Strand and ducks down a side street. In his briefcase is a document written in the ornate copperplate script favoured by the Albion Mutual Providence Society, where he is employed as senior manager. It is a life insurance policy in the name of Mrs Josie Smith of 23A Cunningham Gardens, SW1. The policy was taken out on her behalf by her husband, who signed it, dated it and paid over the sum of £8.

All ship-shape and above board.

Except that neither of the Smiths actually exist. They are a figment of Harbinger's extremely devious mind. Eschewing the riskier money-making routes of the gambling dens or cards, he has devised a far more lucrative way of augmenting his salary. Some might call him a criminal, but if they did, he would refute this hotly. He is a businessman, the difference between a criminal and a businessman being that the businessman has imagination.

The scam works like this: upon Mrs Smith's demise, the policy will be redeemed, paying out, upon maturity, the sum of £200. It is the money he needs to buy into his pal Carstairs' latest enterprise, and he hopes it will convince Carstairs that he is worth the status of a joint partnership.

All Arthur Harbinger requires now is Mrs Smith's death certificate, signed and dated by a member of the medical profession. Or a medical student in need of funds. There are always such people, if one knows where to look. And he does. Harbinger is on his way to collect a death certificate from a doctor who isn't a doctor, for a woman who never existed.

*****

On their return to Scotland Yard, Jack Cully dispatches the young constable to his next duties. Then he drafts a *'Scotland Yard: Information sought'* advertisement to be circulated to all the police offices. Cully knows this is a risky undertaking as it frequently elicits a steady stream of Londoners all willing to 'help the police with their inquiries', which translated means hindering them as much as possible by false sightings, fake confessions and misleading information.

Nevertheless. Somewhere out there, in the teeming tenements or stately squares, there must be somebody who can identify the deceased and now missing man. A wife, a friend, a landlady or work colleague? Who was the last person to see him alive? Once the police know that, they can work backwards to discover why he died, and why his body was stolen from the police mortuary.

Having prepared his notice, Cully sets out once more on his travels. He is taking the half-smoked cigar to a nearby tobacconist to see what he can find out. He heads towards Mr Leonidas' Superior Tobacco & Sweet Shop, where he is a regular customer. Both Cully's small daughters are partial to sweeties, and he often calls in on his way home to buy a bag of something for them to share.

Cully pushes open the door. The bell tinkles brightly, bringing Mr Leonidas hurrying over to the counter. He has been arranging various glass jars full of brightly coloured sweets. His face lights up with a welcoming smile when he spies his customer.

"Detective Mr Cully! It is you! Welcome to my little emporium. Now then, what can I offer you today? Look in the cabinet ~ I have some lovely strawberry creams, fresh in ~ the little ones, they would like them very much, I think. Yes?"

Cully agrees that they would indeed. "But that is not why I am here, Mr Leonidas," he says, drawing the cigar stub from his inside pocket. "What can you tell me about this?" he says, laying it on the counter.

The tobacconist picks up the cigar, studies it, turns it, sniffs it. "It is a figurado," he says. Then, seeing Cully's puzzled expression, he goes on. "It is made out of a combination of tobaccos ~ very difficult to produce, and in consequence, very expensive." He studies the band closely. "Cuaba ~ not a brand I stock here, Detective Mr Cully. Not even a brand I know. This is a very up-market cigar, the sort that a rich aristocratic gentleman might enjoy."

"And where might he purchase one?"

Mr Leonidas shrugs. "That I cannot tell you. I am sorry. Maybe you should inquire at the tobacco warehouse in the London Docks. They should have a list of the places they supply with this type of cigar." He eyes Cully narrowly. "Is this to do with one of your investigations, Detective Mr Cully?"

Cully nods.

"Ah. I see. Then I hope it is successful. If not, you can probably get 10d on the street for a half-smoked cigar of this quality."

Cully smiles. "I'll certainly bear it in mind. Thanks for your help, Mr Leonidas."

As Cully turns to go, Mr Leonidas holds up a forefinger, indicating that he should wait. Then, as Cully watches, the shopkeeper picks up a small silver shovel, opens the glass-fronted display case on the counter and scoops a couple of pink strawberry creams into a twist of paper. He holds it out to Cully. "For the little ones. No, please, no charge. It is a gift."

Cully voices his thanks.

"Please ~ my pleasure," the Greek shop owner says. "And I shall ask my compatriots about the cigar. Maybe one of them might know something. If they do, I shall send you word."

****

Emily Cully, wife of Jack Cully and owner of a successful dressmaking business, has got her hands full. Throughout the early summer months, she and her team of outworkers (all paid properly), have been working their fingers almost to the bone to produce the one-off light gauzy silk and satin tea dresses and ball gowns required by the clients of the up-market fashion stores they supply. No ready-made for these belles; their mamas have the money to pay for exclusivity, even if the beautiful gowns will only be worn once before being wrapped in cotton and placed in a trunk in the attic.

Now, with Autumn and Winter in mind, the same stores are requesting clothes in heavier fabrics, which are laborious to run up in hot weather. Emily is toiling over a jabot in figured velvet ~ a difficult material to work with, as it creeps. As she pushes herself to a stand, placing her hand against the base of her spine to ease the ache there, she reminds herself that before the invention of that marvel, the sewing machine, she'd have been hand-stitching much of the jacket, sitting at a wooden table in a long room in the dimly lit basement of a shop, watched over by a bullying overseer.

Emily pauses at the window, letting her mind drift back to her youth, when she was Emily Benet and, with her best friend Violet Manning, had come to London to make their fortunes sewing beautiful dresses for rich ladies. How full of hopes and dreams they were. How young and naive. She remembers Violet's horrific murder, her body dumped in an alleyway. The bitter heartbreak that followed her friend's death, the long hours bent over her needle, the starvation wages leading to her collapse at work.

She had been rescued by a kind workmate and fed back into life, and love, for it was through the tragedy of Violet's murder that she met her husband, Jack Cully, who had been investigating the crime. Theirs has been a happy marriage of equals. Not a day passes when Emily doesn't count her blessings. Two of them are currently under the table, playing with some empty bobbins.

Emily glances at the clock. It is nearly time for Jack's return home. There is a succulent chicken pie browning in the oven, and the tiny garden has yielded fat orange carrots and a few potatoes to accompany it. She bends down and peers under the work-table.

"Violet, Primmy, Father will be home soon. If you fetch your bonnets, we can all walk to meet him."

The girls rush to obey their mother and the little cavalcade soon sets out. Primrose is a slow and unpractised walker, tending to get diverted by stones, cracks in the pavement and weeds, so she is carried along by her sister. Emily regards her oldest daughter with satisfaction. Violet is doing well at the small school she attends. Her reading is fluent, thanks to her father who, since her birth, has always read aloud to her out of whatever discarded newspaper he finds in Stride's office. She writes a neat hand and has shown an aptitude for figures.

Emily hopes Violet has a bright future ahead of her. Certainly not one of drudgery, eking out the pennies and wondering where the next meal will come from. That is not what she wants for her daughter. Emily has, in her secret drawer, a cutting from a newspaper advertising the opening of a girls' public day school. She has been putting bits of her earnings aside regularly ever since Violet was born, against the day when she will be old enough to apply.

Turning the corner of the street, she spots the familiar figure in the distance. Emily waves, while the two little girls spring along the pavement, love giving their small feet wings. Jack Cully catches Primrose and tosses her into the air, to screams of delight. He ruffles Violet's curls, then greets Emily with a smile.

"Now, there's a welcome! Perhaps there is something in my pocket for you both? I wonder if there is?"

Violet dips her hand into his jacket pocket and lifts out the strawberry creams. Her eyes sparkle.

"Look mama! Sweets! Papa has sweets! I'm definitely going to be a detective when I grow up ~ you get given so many sweeties!"

Jack Cully smiles indulgently over the top of her head, while Emily calmly transfers the little bag to her own pocket. "You can enjoy them after your supper, Vi, not before. I don't want you spoiling your appetite."

The little family walks the short distance to their home. Violet chatters on about the sums she got right. Primrose bounces up and down in her father's arms. Emily's thoughts run ahead to the meal she is about to dish up. It is her favourite part of the day: the family seated round the table that doubles as a work space. Heads bent over their plates. And after the dishes have been washed and tidied, and the girls put to bed, Jack Cully lights his pipe and regales her with aspects of the current investigation, or Stride's latest outburst, or else he reads to her from the newspaper while she sews.

Tonight follows the same familiar routine. Cully talks about his visit to the tobacconist and describes the young constable whose written report has impressed the two older detectives. Emily sits in the opposite chair, her hands busily smocking a tiny dress. Gradually, Cully's attention becomes focused on what she is doing.

"I thought you weren't making any more baby clothes for a while, Em. So ~ who is the sewing for?" His eyes suddenly widen. "Don't say you are ..."

Emily Cully shakes her head and laughs. "Your face, Jack! It's a picture! No, this is for somebody else's child. A close friend of mine and a colleague of yours. There now, I have given you all the 'clues' you need to solve it. Can you guess who?"

A look of puzzlement crosses Cully's face. Then, enlightenment dawns. "You don't mean, surely ..."

"Yes, Josephine and Lachlan Grieg are expecting a baby. He may not have told you yet, but I knew it as soon as I saw her a few weeks ago ~ a woman always does know these things. Please pretend to be very surprised when you find out."

"I shall genuinely be very delighted!" Jack Cully exclaims. "Lachlan is one of the finest inspectors I have ever worked with. What wonderful news! But, will she have to give up working once the baby arrives?"

"Oh, I am sure she won't. Josephine will find some way to carry on her business, one way or another. After all, as she always says, 'if a queen can run a country, why can't a woman run a company?'"

Detective Sergeant Jack Cully has been happily married for many years, during which time he has learned an awful lot about women. Mainly, he has learned there is a time to speak and a time to remain silent. This is one of the latter times. Therefore, he makes no comment. He wouldn't dare.

****

After their visit to Aunt Euphemia comes to an end, Sherborne Harbinger and his son return to their hotel rooms, where the success of the visit is described in glowing terms to Harriet and her mother. Following a disappointing luncheon in the hotel dining-room, the family sallies forth, Bradshaw in hand, to see some of the sights of London. They visit the British Museum, and view various statues of famous men, for Harbinger is determined that Hanover must be exposed to man's greatest achievements, to give every opportunity for some of it to rub off onto him.

A request from Harriet to see 'some statues of famous women' is treated with dismissive scorn by the male members of the party, and after partaking of tea and cakes at a small tea-room, they return to their hotel once more, where Sherborne Harbinger writes to his older brother to announce his arrival in the city and request an urgent meeting to discuss Aunt Euphemia and their mutual interest in her timely demise.

Dinner is a rather silent affair, punctuated by sharp parental requests to the twins to keep their elbows off the table and not to slurp their soup. At the termination of the meal, Hanover and Harriet and the baby are dispatched to their respective rooms to prepare for bed, supervised by their mother.

As soon as they have gone, Sherborne orders a brandy, lights up a pipe and eases back into a comfortable chair. There is much to think about, mainly how to sound out his brother at their meeting on the morrow. The two have not met face to face for some time, although letters of an accusatory and unsatisfactory nature have been exchanged. At last, as the clock strikes nine, he declares to his beloved that he will take a turn about the streets before bed.

The streets of London at night are a revelation. Crowds of men and women push past him on the narrow pavements, all set upon finding pleasure in some form or another. The yellow glare from shop-windows streams out into the warm, murky air, throwing a shifting radiance across the thronged thoroughfare.

There is something eerie and ghost-like about the endless procession of faces that flit from gloom into light and back into gloom again. On every corner, brightly-lit public houses beckon with their brassy signs and raucous bonhomie. Eventually finding himself in an insalubrious part of town, Sherborne decides, on a whim, to enter a music hall.

It is not the sort of place he would usually attend, but after a day of educational sight-seeing with his sullen offspring, he feels a sudden unaccustomed desire to be among the common people and share vicariously in their simple, if vulgar, pleasures. If nothing else, it reminds him of how superior his own life is. And, hopefully, it is about to become even more superior. Harbinger settles himself at a table close to the stage, orders a drink and prepares to be disapprovingly entertained.

****

Let us step back a few hours. Having safely collected and banked the life insurance money from his fictitious client, Arthur Harbinger dismisses his clerk and closes down his desk at the Albion Mutual Providence Society. He then prepares himself for the evening ahead. Supper must be secured first of course, for Harbinger is a confirmed bachelor, preferring to shift for himself. Women, he has observed, come with a lot of bag and baggage. Ditto dresses, bonnets, shoes and other items of finery that empty the male purse.

Not for him the pleasant fireside, the doting ministrations of some Angel in the House, the patter of small childish feet, or the clutch of sticky infant hands. A solitary life means he makes his own decisions, chooses his own path, be it straight or crooked, and owes allegiance to no one, which suits him just fine.

Harbinger sets his face westward, and after a short walk, arrives at one of the pleasant eating-houses that surround the theatres and cater for those who do not choose to dine in a public house surrounded by loud noise. He selects a mutton chop with vegetables and a good claret to accompany it. Tempted, he ends his meal with a raspberry tart. Back on the street once more, replete and satisfied, he saunters back to his bachelor apartment.

The fetid London air seems to have had all the goodness breathed out of it. Even the flâneurs seem languid and almost indifferent to their surroundings. Harbinger plans to spend the hours until bedtime smoking his pipe and reading the evening newspapers.

But before this can happen, there is a letter on the mantelpiece awaiting his attention. He recognises the familiar handwriting of his younger brother Sherborne. With a sigh, he slits open the envelope and extracts the sheet of cheapish writing paper. As he reads, the frown between his eyebrows deepens and his jaw tightens.

One of the main benefits for Harbinger of his almost hermetic existence is the severance of all familial ties. The last time he saw his brother and younger sister was at the funeral of their father. He has exchanged correspondence with Sherborne upon business matters concerning the paternal Will and such like, but he has not set eyes upon him since that day, although he has made sure he is kept abreast of what his brother gets up to. Of his sister, he has no knowledge whatsoever, other than the recollection of a slender young woman dressed in black, snuffling in an unattractive way under a veil, while some clergyman told lies about the closeness of their family.

But now, his relatives must come crashing into his world, unasked and unwelcome. He will be forced to be agreeable to people he does not care about, fawn upon children he regards with disapprobation. He has spent the past few weeks carefully cultivating Aunt Euphemia Harbinger, with an eye to inheriting her considerable wealth. He did not imagine that she would go behind his back and write to Sherborne and Wilhelmina.

If only he had suspected her intentions, he might have saved her the trouble by informing her that both siblings had perished in a fire. Or a train crash. Or had emigrated. Arthur Harbinger takes up his pen and with a weary sigh of resignation, replies to his brother's letter. Resentment seethes through every line and by the end of the short missive, it is as much as he can do to sign his name. He thrusts the letter into his pocket and heads out to find the nearest post box, muttering a curse upon the recipient as he does so.

****

Night wears on until eventually, dawn arrives. It is a bright summer morning, and the clocks of the city are all striking nine as Miss Lucy Landseer, a handsome young woman with deep blue eyes and hair the colour of untamed treacle, stands outside Number 122A, Baker Street, admiring the shiny new brass plate that adorns the brickwork. *'L. Landseer, Private Consulting Detective'* it reads, and in lower letters underneath: *'Discretion is our watchword'*. She reaches into her satchel, pulls out a white cotton handkerchief, and gives the brass plate a quick polish.

Then, nodding her approval, she turns the key to Number 122A, Baker Street and lets herself in. The hallway, which is communal, has a shiny side table for business cards and a silver dish to contain them. It also features a couple of chairs for clients to wait, and a grandfather clock that ticks but is always forty-three minutes late. The black and white floor tiles are spotless, for Mr Macready, who owns the building and rents out rooms, is a stickler for cleanliness, which is, in his opinion, on an even higher plane than Godliness.

It was one of the things that made Lucy decide to set up her business here. That and the proximity of Baker Street underground station. Clients needed to feel that they were visiting a respectable person who would help them solve their problems and first impressions were vital for establishing this. Plus, the closeness of the underground meant that they could arrive and slip away discreetly.

Lucy Landseer mounts the stairs to the first floor, stopping before a door labelled '**Consulting Room**'. Here she is. She unlocks the door and enters, untying her bonnet and hanging it on one of the wall pegs, along with her outdoor coat. A shaft of pale morning sunlight slides in, painting the desk, the typing machine, the letter rack, the cliental chair (gold painted and padded with crimson

29

velvet), her own chair (wooden and unpadded) and the portrait of some august female worthy whom she discovered in one of the small curio shops opposite the British Museum. She sits down on her chair, places her elbows on her desk and rests her small chin in her cupped hands.

Lucy Landseer has come a very long way from the wide-eyed young woman, barely out of her teens, who arrived in the great city of London with sufficient funds to support herself for a year. But Lucy's plan, to make a living as a writer, has succeeded beyond her wildest dreams. Writing as the *Silver Quill*, her witty observations on London life won her a regular column in *All the Year Round*, and praise from its famous editor. This was followed by her first novel, a sensational tale of foreign love and tragedy (about which she knew nothing), which garnered some good reviews.

But it is her latest venture that has prompted her to set up in business on her own. A monthly series of stories featuring Belle Batchelor, the daring female private detective, and her faithful canine sidekick Harris, have caught the public imagination to such an extent that the publishing house has been regularly inundated with letters pleading for Belle's help in solving various personal problems.

On the day the Metropolitan Police had to be called to clear the crowd of desperate suppliants from its door, her publisher suggested, slightly tongue-in-cheek, that Miss Landseer should consider setting up as a real female private detective as she obviously had a talent for it. It was meant as an ironic comment, but the remark struck a chord deep inside her.

Over supper with her Cambridge professor (the man she shares a house with, but isn't married to quite yet), the chord became a full-blown symphony. Premises were quickly sought. Furniture rapidly hired. Business cards speedily commissioned, and advertisements placed in all the most and some of the less most respectable newspapers.

And now here she is. The chimneys breathe out songs of smoke, the horses' hooves strike the cobbles in response, the cries of street-sellers twine and writhe like strings of bright beads. The world is full of sounds and wonder. And, if she is not mistaken, a carriage has just pulled up outside.

Lucy clasps her hands together as she waits to see who alights from the carriage, and whether they have come to consult her, the draper downstairs, or the bespoke dressmaker who occupies the floor above. She does not have to wait long. The doorbell rings. There is a pattering of feet as the little maid who is employed to sweep, clean the front step, and answer the door, performs one of her duties.

She hears the dulcet, low tones of a woman. Then footsteps climb the stairs and halt outside her door. There is a light knock. Lucy rises and goes to greet her first client, a heavily veiled woman dressed in full mourning.

"Am I addressing Miss Landseer, the private detective?" she inquires, in a pleasant voice.

"I am indeed she. Pray enter," Lucy says, standing aside to let her visitor walk into the consulting room. A pleasant scent of lavender rises from the woman's skirts as she passes.

"Please sit down and tell me what has brought you here," Lucy says, drawing a brand-new notebook towards her and choosing a pen from the tray. "I promise I will do my best to help you."

The woman sighs. Then she lifts her veil, revealing a pale, youthful face, with deep-set eyes under strongly-marked black brows. Her forehead is clouded and her expression one of haunting sadness.

"My name is Rosalind Whitely, and my story is simply told, Miss Landseer. As you see, I am in mourning. It has been six months since my beloved mother passed from this earth to a better world. She endured much suffering: a cruel disease took its toll of her body, but she bore it bravely.

"My father, who was a saint on earth, died some years previously. I am an only child, Miss Landseer, and so the care of my mother has been my sole preoccupation since his sudden and tragic demise. We were very close and shared everything. Our lives were entwined together: we read aloud to each other, worked upon our various sewing tasks in the evening and it was my joy to provide tasty meals in an effort to coax her to eat.

"You see how we were all in all to each other? But that idyllic time was to change. Last year, her doctor recommended the waters at Bath, which are supposed to be good for rheumatism. My mother, in the company of a nurse, left London for a sojourn there to try the treatment for herself. I remained here to oversee the house and the servants.

"Imagine my emotions when, out of the blue, I received a letter from my mother stating that she had met a gentleman ~ and that they were engaged to be married!" The young woman swallows and grips her hands together convulsively. "It was a very sudden and whirlwind courtship, Miss Landseer. I saw my mother off on the train with a paid nurse and one of our maids. Six weeks later, she came back married to my stepfather. He was a widower, considerably younger, who had also gone to Bath to take the waters. I confess that I was bewildered, but I tried to swallow my feelings for her sake.

"They seemed perfectly happy together, and I could not fault his attention to her, but naturally, his presence in the house meant that our former intimacy lapsed, and

I was forced to rely on my own company in the evenings, for I did not care to sit with them. Sadly, a few months after her return to London, my mother's health began to fail once more. I was absent from the house, so not able to comfort her in her final moments and I shall have to live the rest of my life with the guilt of that upon my conscience."

"I am very sorry that you have been left to bear this burden on your own," Lucy says. "May I enquire where you were at the time of her death?"

"I was visiting the seaside," the young woman answers. "It was suggested by her doctor that, as her health had not improved after her sojourn at Bath, some sea air might be good for Mama. I had gone down to Torquay to select a suitable hotel and make arrangements for her stay there. When I returned, it was to discover that she had been dead for three days." She bows her head and sighs.

"You were not to know that her death would follow so soon after your departure, Miss Whitely," Lucy says. "I fear none of us can predict such an event."

"But I should not have left the house!" the young woman exclaims. "My stepfather, Mr Brooke, persuaded me to go. He said that a woman would be better placed to select the right hotel, to ask the right questions about accommodation, the provision of invalid fare. He also assured me that my mother was in the best medical hands in London."

Ah. The stepfather again. Lucy circles the words thoughtfully.

"Do you suspect foul play, Miss Whitely? Is that the reason you are consulting me?"

The client wrings her hands, her mouth moving tremulously. "I do not know what I suspect, Miss Landseer. My thoughts whirl around in my head. I have nothing to accuse Mr Brooke of directly. Nothing at all.

My mother seemed perfectly happy to be married to him. I never heard a cross word pass between them. Nothing I could reproach him with, although the loss of our previous closeness was a hard blow for me to bear. And yet …"

"You wish to be reassured that her death was from natural causes and could not have been aided or hastened by any human intervention, is that it?"

"Yes. Yes. That is what I want to find out. I feel that my life cannot continue upon its way until I am at peace over her final days in London. I have such dreadful thoughts …"

"Then I shall do my best to set your mind at ease," Lucy says firmly, adding, "it might aid me in my investigation if I could visit your house ~ the investigating mind works better when it can see the actual places in which events occurred." (She has read this somewhere.)

"Yes, of course, Miss Landseer. I quite understand your request. My stepfather leaves for his office every morning at nine. I usually perform various household tasks after he has left and spend my afternoons in varied domestic pursuit. If you care to call upon me any afternoon, I shall be delighted to welcome you, and answer any further questions you wish to ask me."

"Then it shall be so," Lucy says. She rises, proffers her hand, and shows her client to the communal stairs.

Once the front door has closed, Lucy Landseer returns to her desk to write up her notes. Writing up notes is an integral part of the investigative process. She opens her brand-new notebook, picks up her brand-new pen, and in her best handwriting, writes: *Case Number 1: The Suspicious Stepfather.*

****

34

While Lucy Landseer is busily engaged with her first client, across town in Mrs Cordelia Brimmer's lodging-house (Clean Beds. Mangling Done), breakfast is being served. Porridge steams in a large pot, despite the summer heat, and hunks of day-old bread are cut up and piled on a cracked platter.

Mrs Brimmer's lodgers belong to the class of individuals for whom fear of hunger is always present, so anything that fills their stomachs is welcome. They sit around a wooden table in the small back kitchen, with wet washing piled in baskets and draped on racks over their heads, consuming lumpy porridge, with the occasional drip from the clothes hung above falling into their bowls to flavour it.

There are currently four people lodging with Mrs Brimmer: George Spiner, Jewish, a shirt maker, John Denny, who works in a halfpenny shaving shop, and Micky Mokey and Little Azella, music hall artists, who have come to London for the summer season, and share a small room together on the top floor.

Micky Mokey is a slender young individual in his early twenties, always dapper in his attire, with a habit of thrusting his hands deep into his trouser pockets and whistling under his breath. His skin is smooth and beardless, and he wears his dark curly hair parted on one side and just a little too long. ("Them music hall people is a bit bourgwoir for my taste," says Mrs Brimmer to her neighbour).

Little Azella, as her name suggests, is a tiny female of uncertain age, fond of appearing at the breakfast table in spangly frocks, with a faded pink velvet rose tucked behind one ear. She is an acrobat and female gymnast. He sings popular songs. They both currently appear thrice nightly at the Varieties Music Hall in Bishopsgate Street.

It is assumed by the other lodgers and their landlady, from their closeness, shared hair-colour and a tendency to finish off each other's sentences, that the two are brother and sister. It is assumed incorrectly. Breakfast over, they return to their room, where Little Azella packs her tights, her sparkly vest, her chalk and her shoes, bids her companion a cheery farewell, and sets off to rehearse.

Meanwhile, Micky Mokey thrusts his hands into his trouser pockets and stares gloomily into the fly-blown looking glass. He frowns. Last night, while belting out that popular music hall ditty *'You don't have to be a lady to be my bestest gal'* in his pleasant light tenor voice, a member of the audience sitting in the pit had suddenly caught his eye. Somebody he had not seen for a very long time. It was all Micky Mokey could do to hold the tune and get to the final verse without drying.

As soon as the chairman had banged his gavel to usher him off the stage, Micky Mokey had fled to the tiny dressing-room shared with whoever else was on the bill. There he had shucked off his stage costume, donned his street clothes and hurried out into the airless night.

Of all the music halls, in all the cities, in all the country, he had to walk into mine, he'd thought ruefully, as he set off back to his lodgings. It was an omen. Though whether of good or ill, he could not yet tell.

****

Detective Inspector Stride is struggling to get to work. It is another blazing hot day, and the streets are like an oven. The glare of sunlight from the new staring yellow-brick buildings is almost painful to the eye. Hard to believe that these are the same streets that loomed so gloomily during the fogs of winter. He passes a news-stand and is gratified to see that no morning paper is featuring a 'Mysterious Theft of Dead Body from Police Mortuary' story, which means that *The Inquirer* must be still unaware of it.

Stride enters Scotland Yard, once again minus his usual mug of hot, strong, black coffee. As he passes the Anxious Bench, where members of the public wait to hear news of their nearest and dearest, who have been arrested for crimes *they did not commit*, a familiar figure rises lazily and hails him.

"Wotcher Stride. I hear you recently lost a dead body. Bit careless, eh?"

Damn. Just when he was congratulating himself on the story not escaping. Stride feels a frisson of dislike run through him as he turns to face Richard Dandy, known colloquially as Dandy Dick, chief reporter on *The Inquirer*, a thorn in the side of the detective division and his own particular nemesis.

"*Detective Inspector* Stride, *Mr* Dandy," he replies stiffly. "As you well know. And is there a reason for your visit?"

Dandy Dick smirks. "Just doing my job. Asking questions, getting answers. I thought I'd stop by and inquire, on behalf of the Man in the Street, who pays your wages, by the way, whether it had turned up yet. The body. That you lost. Because from where I'm standing, it's not so much the forces of law and order, as the farces of law and order. Ha ha. So, has it? Turned up?"

Stride grinds his teeth and spins on his heel.

"I'll take that as a 'no', then," Dandy Dick calls after him. "Watch out for my piece in the evening edition. It'll make a nice little story. 'Dead Man Escapes the Clutches of Criminally Careless Cops!'"

Stride turns, his face red with fury. "Don't you dare …" he begins, but Dandy Dick has already left. Stride glares at the desk constable, who is yet another member of the new intake and so unfamiliar with how things work *viz-a-viz* members of the fifth estate.

"Have you been talking to that individual?" he demands.

The shifty look on the constable's face provides him with the answer. Stride groans inwardly. "If he ever tries to set foot inside Scotland Yard again, you are to arrest him. Do you understand?"

"Yes sir. Of course, sir. On what charge, sir?" asks the constable.

"For being a total waste of my time," Stride growls. "Look, when Detective Sergeant Cully comes in, tell him I'd like a word, would you? And in the meantime, don't talk to any newspaper men who breeze in here asking questions. Ever."

Stride steams his way to his office, where he throws stuff around his desk in an attempt to calm himself down. After a while, he settles and begins drafting a stern memo to all members of the police force, reminding them that they are not to give any interviews to any members of the press without consulting him first.

By the time Jack Cully knocks at his office door, Stride has worked through a couple of drafts, and finally come up with a copy that satisfies him and doesn't contain too much invective.

"Read this," he says, waving a sheet of paper at Cully. "Do you know, I actually caught Richard Dandy in the front office this morning, trying to get information about that missing body out of the new constable. The very idea! We simply can't allow penny-a-liners like that just to walk in and start interviewing random members of the police force. Who knows where it will end?"

"Indeed," Cully murmurs. He reads Stride's instructions, mentally re-phrasing some sentences and toning down various paragraphs. "I'll get someone to type this up and make copies of it for you, shall I?"

Stride fans himself with one of the discarded drafts. "I hate this weather, Jack. It's too hot. It's not natural ~ I can't think in this heat," he complains. "Has anyone come forward to identify the wretched man? No? Why not? People are usually keen as mustard to stick their noses into police business. The sooner we know who he was, the sooner we can stop people like Dandy Dick writing their rubbish and making our lives difficult."

Cully demurs. Since finding the half-smoked cigar, he has moved away from the need to identify the missing man. The ability to lead an investigation often means knowing when to shift tactics. Cully's tactics have shifted. Now, he is more focused on discovering who the man might have been with, rather than who he was.

Carefully, he explains his new strategy to Stride. Cully knows his colleague of old, and knows that, like some giant steel ship, Stride is difficult to turn around once he has set off, so to prepare the groundwork, he describes his early morning visit to the Docks, accompanied by young Constable Tom Williams.

The two men had gone down to the vast warehouse for the reception of tobacco. It was the first time the young officer had visited the London Docks. Cully recalls his astonished expression as they drew near and saw the forest of masts, and tall chimneys belching out black smoke.

They had picked their way through open streets, lined with low lodging-houses inhabited by dock labourers, watermen, sailors, and the poor who made a precarious living by or from the waterside. They passed shops stocked entirely with gear for sailors: brass sextants, quadrants, chronometers, ropes smelling of tar, bright red and blue flannel shirts, pilot coats and canvas trousers. It seemed every public house they passed had some crude variant of a Jolly Jack Tar upon its painted board.

Eventually Cully had hailed a passing Customs-house officer, distinguished by his brass-buttoned jacket from the sailor population that swarmed the street, and he had directed them to the Customs office, where their inquiries had been met with some initial scepticism, until Cully explained the purpose of their visit, whereupon various large customs books had been opened and consulted, and a list of the suppliers had been handed over.

Once they had got what they came for, the two made their way back to the dock gates, where they passed through the vast crowd of men of all types, ages and grades, waiting hopefully for a day's paid employment unloading one of the great ships.

Having listened in silence, Stride pulls a face. "That's a bit of a long shot, isn't it?"

"Possibly," Cully nods. "But these tobacconists know their customers. Know their likes and dislikes. If we can get a few names, we can make some discreet inquiries, shake a few trees as it were, and see what falls out. The place where the body was discovered is far too out of the way for anybody to be there by accident. Especially somebody who has a taste for smoking very exclusive cigars."

Stride spreads his hands. "Do whatever you think best. But I repeat my initial comment: this is a waste of time. You would be far better off making inquiries around the neighbourhood to see if anybody noticed a couple of suspicious characters with a cart lurking round the back of Scotland Yard on the night when the body was taken."

"Perhaps you are right. Let us see. I shall try both approaches. In the meantime, it is providing our young constable with some invaluable training. And, at the end of the day, it's not as if we are inundated with other cases, is it? People commit far fewer crimes when the weather is as hot as this and so many smaller shops are boarded up for the summer."

Stride agrees. "It is like a desert out there, that's true. Any day now, I expect to turn a corner and see a row of camels making their way along the thoroughfare, or a pyramid rising above the river."

Cully departs, leaving Stride to fill in some rosters in lacklustre fashion until it is time for luncheon. But here again, the weather has conspired against him, for Sally, the eponymous owner of Sally's Chop House ('all meat guaranteed fresh and mainly from recognisable farm animals') has taken off for cooler climes with his family, meaning Stride is served by a musty elderly woman labouring under a chronic sniff.

His beer arrives flat, his chop is flabby, the potato has a hard, uncooked centre and the walls seem to sweat something greasy and unpleasant. Stride sits alone in his customary back booth, finishing his luncheon, and missing the cut and thrust of his daily debate with Sally, so it is a disgruntled detective inspector who returns to his office sometime later, where he sits on discontentedly, doing paperwork until the end of the day. Then he walks home through the baking streets, the air still unbreathable, the sky still painfully blue, finding no pleasure in his own city.

****

Pleasure is a quality that can be found in many places or situations. For instance: *'how good and pleasant it is,'* says the Bible, *'for brothers to dwell in unity.'* Alas, the only unity possessed by Arthur and Sherborne Harbinger is a unity of purpose, and it comes in the form of guineas and paper notes with an image of the Queen upon them.

Here are the unified brethren, gathered on the front step of Aunt Euphemia's house, waiting for the servant to let them in. One man carries a small bunch of flowers, purchased from a small flower-seller on the corner of Tottenham Court Road; the other man bears a basket of fruit. Both eye their brother's gift with disapproval.

"I shouldn't think she'd be able to eat any of that stuff," Arthur sneers, indicating the small pineapple. "The elderly don't like fruit. Disagrees with them."

"Buttercups?" Sherborne responds. *"Buttercups? Really?"*

"A reminder of her happy childhood in the countryside. A simple flower to bring back sweet memories of roaming the yellow fields as an infant, plucking nature's bounty from the green bosom of the earth."

"I thought she was born in Highgate."

The front door is opened. Arthur Harbinger shoots his brother a venomous glare, and steps quickly across the threshold, blocking the doorway. He hands his coat, hat and silver-topped stick to Rose, the stern-faced housekeeper, then strides towards the sitting room, leaving his brother to follow him a few seconds later.

"Miss Harbinger is writing her letters," Rose says primly. "I shall tell her you are here."

Sherborne crosses the room to the window and removes the cover from the parrot cage. The parrot shakes its head, then sidles hopefully along its perch.

"Wotcher me old cock," it says. *"Polly wants a biscuit. Where's Harriet? Good Poll. Remember what I told you?"*

"What in Heaven's name is THAT?" Arthur exclaims.

"A little gift to aunt from my family," Sherborne says loftily. "The elderly need taking out of themselves. We thought the bird might cheer her up in her last days. And it will allow my boy to make regular visits to help look after it. Nothing like the presence of a delightful small child to remind an elderly relative of her duties."

Arthur Harbinger snorts derisively. "You always were a lost cause, Sherborne. No wonder father favoured me."

"He did not!" his brother retorts hotly. "He once told me he thought that you would never amount to anything much."

Arthur laughs heartily at the suggestion. "Oh, little brother, still playing that old tune? What a desperate soul it is!"

Sherborne's hands bunch into tight fists. "I am a successful man of business. I have a nice home, a devoted wife and three children. You have nothing. Nothing!"

Arthur Harbinger folds his arms and stares at him, a smile spreading slowly across his lean features, his eyes empty as water.

"And that's why you're here, desperately trying to ingratiate yourself with Aunt E. isn't it? Successful man of business? Living beyond your income is more like it ~ oh I know all about you, little brother. The expensive house, the hired carriage ~ it's all a front, isn't it? You are up to your eyebrows in hock to your bank, and if Aunt E. don't leave you a fortune, which she ain't going to, by the way, you can kiss goodbye to the fine house, and the rest."

Sherborne utters a howl of rage, which is instantly subsumed into a cough, as the housekeeper re-enters the room.

"My mistress will see you both now," she says. "Briefly."

The two men stampede up the stairs, almost elbowing each other aside to enter the front bedroom where Aunt Euphemia is sitting up in bed, swathed in a lacy shawl, a portable writing desk propped up in front of her. Despite the heat of the day, the windows are closed, the curtains half-looped. The room smells of lavender water and old lady.

"Aunty," coos Sherborne, "How wonderful to see you this morning. And how well you look. Does she not, Arthur?"

Arthur Sherborne bestows a smile of ghastly unctuousness upon the pinched-faced stick-figure in the bed. He lays the bunch of buttercups on the writing-desk.

"A little offering from the countryside, dear aunt."

The old woman brushes them aside. "Rose ~ for goodness' sake ~ take these away at once; they are spilling pollen upon my letters!"

Sherborne sneaks a sly grin as the maid removes the flowers. "Here is some fresh fruit for you, Aunty Euphemia. I rose at the crack of dawn to go to Covent Garden to purchase it."

The old woman frowns. "What is that?" she asks, extending a shaky claw and pointing to the pineapple on top of the fruit pile.

"A lovely pine. My dear children adore it."

"Then let them eat it. I can't stomach fruit. Never could. Take it back with you."

She sinks back upon the pillows, her dark beady eyes travelling from one man's face to the other. "Where's the third one of you?" she demands.

The brothers exchange puzzled glances.

"The girl. Or rather, the young woman, as I guess she is now. I wrote to her. Haven't had a reply yet. Where's she? Why isn't she here, with her calculator and her empty bag, waiting for her share of my money?"

Enlightenment dawns.

"Oh, you mean sister Wilhelmina," Arthur Harbinger says smoothly. "She is not able to travel to London at the moment."

"Of course, we intend to share any good fortune that might possibly happen to come our way with her," Sherborne interjects. "She is our sister, our flesh and blood after all."

The lie is almost palpable.

"I liked her," Aunt Euphemia mutters. "Had some pluck about her, I recall. I want to see her again before I die. I have some bits and pieces of family jewellery I'd like to give her." She stares up at them fiercely. "You remind her of my letter and ask her to come and see me. And you'd better be quick about it; my doctor tells me he doesn't think I'm long for this world, and I have no reason to distrust his judgement. Now go, I've had quite enough of the pair of you."

Arthur makes a small formal bow. "We'll leave you in peace then, dear aunt," he says, then inquires casually, "Shall I post those letters for you on my way to the City? It would be a pleasure to serve you."

The old woman indicates graciously that he may do so. Arthur picks up the two letters and without reading the addresses, tucks them straight into his pocket. The brothers slink out of the room.

"Do you know where Wilhelmina is?" Sherborne asks, as they descend the stairs.

Arthur shakes his head. "Last time I saw her was at the pater's funeral. You?"

Sherborne frowns. "Me too. I can't remember seeing her since. It has been so many years since we met. She wasn't there for the reading of the Will, was she? I'm sure I'd remember if she was."

Neither brother will ever admit that they could have helped their sister out with some of the money they inherited upon the death of their parent. After all, it was not their responsibility. The childhood home, the furniture, money and other things, had been left to them jointly, with the option of sharing with their sister. It was an option they mutually declined to take up.

"Well, I do not intend to write to Wilhelmina now," Arthur says. "And nor should you. The last thing we need is for our sister to turn up out of the blue and steal our rightful inheritance from under our noses. I shall tell aunt that I am making diligent enquiries, of course. But I won't be."

The brothers part company on the doorstep. Sherborne sets out for the hotel, where his wife and three children await his return and, in Harriet's case, news of Poll. Arthur turns his face towards the City. The letters, however, remain in his pocket; they are not for posting. Later, after his day's work is done, he will steam open the envelopes, read the contents, reassuring himself that they do not involve any Will changes. He'll then trace and copy his aunt's signature on a life insurance policy. It will be backdated to the winter of last year and filed in a drawer in the office, amongst other documents of that time.

A policy taken out for the sum of £100 (half the money he has recently banked) will, upon maturity, pay out a thousand at least. All that remains is for the old lady to die, and, if necessary, he is sure that it can be arranged in such a way that he is not incriminated. *So, Sherborne my little brother,* Arthur thinks, *what will you do to get your hands upon all that lovely money? Perhaps it is time to find out.*

****

It is said of the city of London that in no other place might a man enjoy more undisturbed freedom of thought and rational action, for in London, the individuality of a man is of little consequence; in that strange, crowded jumble of lives that makes up the greatest city on earth, there is little feeling of solidarity or of brotherhood.

Hundreds of thousands of individuals of all classes and ranks of society pack the streets, all restless and hungry for something. People rush past each other as if they had nothing in common. They pass and repass, their quick tread wearing the rough stones smooth and glossy underfoot. In London, a man might fall down in the street and expire, and get no more than a sparing glance from passers-by, and though his absence might be missed by his employer for a day or two, his place would quickly be filled by another.

Thus, when the Honourable Thomas Langland, MP arrives in his parliamentary office and discovers that his private secretary is not at his post once again, he sends for a ministerial aide and requests a replacement.

The Replacement, when he finally arrives, is a short stooping young man, his fair, meagre hair already thinning. He has spectacles and pale blue eyes. He wears a soft collar and cravat and a slightly shiny suit. A man you might pass on your way to the underground station and never notice or think of again. Instantly forgettable.

His appearance, however, belies a mind as sharp as a cook's knife, honed by several years spent quietly getting on with his work while closely observing the political food chain around him. He lives in Kilburn, renting a small room over a shoe shop. He keeps a diary. Such innocuous men are overlooked, frequently misjudged, and always dangerous.

There is also a connection between him and the previous occupant. The Replacement and his predecessor had started in the parliamentary clerks' system on the same day. They were of the same educational background, and so had been drawn to each other's company. But one, thanks to his personal charm, better wardrobe and easy ability to make influential contacts, had speedily risen up the ladder, eventually slipping into the role of Langland's private secretary.

The other, the son of a blacksmith, who grew up holding the bridles of horses and whistling to them to keep them calm, had knocked about in various outlying ministries, a bit like a political docker, turning up each day without knowing who he'd be asked to work for next. An ability to charm horses has proved not to be a transferable skill.

The Honourable MP barely registers his presence. He is an anonymous clerk behind a writing desk. Without even bothering to ask his name, he hands over the draft of a speech he has prepared, requesting that the clerk copies it out in his best hand, making any adjustments he thinks necessary. The Replacement lowers his eyes, selects a pen and commences upon the task in hand.

After an hour, the Honourable MP passes his desk, glances down, nods in a satisfied way, then announces that he is dining at his Club and won't be back until the House sits for the afternoon. The Replacement waits until his footsteps have receded into the distance. Then he sets down his pen and picking up the copied speech, he leaves his desk.

Opening the door to the inner office, the Replacement treads lightly across the crimson carpet and slides into the broad leather-backed desk chair placed directly in front of the portrait of the Queen. So, this is what the inner sanctum of a Member of Parliament looks like? He riffles carefully through the papers on top of the shiny mahogany desk. They seem to consist of committee reports, together with various letters from constituents seeking redress over disputes.

Having satisfied himself that there is nothing of great import to be seen, he moves on to the desk drawers, which yield the customary stationery, bottles of ink and a pen knife, and a number of pamphlets listing various ladies, with their London addresses, scantily clad photographs and descriptions of the services they are prepared to offer the discerning customer.

In the bottom left-hand drawer, he finds a bottle of good brandy, a box of cigars and a small cut-glass tumbler. The right-hand drawer is locked. At which point, he hears voices in the outer office, and the door opens. The Honourable MP and a companion enter the room, bringing with them the blustering bonhomie of a lavish lunch and a waft of cigar smoke.

"I have just this minute put your afternoon speech upon your desk, sir," says the Replacement, who has now moved to stand in front of the desk. He lowers his gaze humbly to the carpet. The very model of a humble civil servant.

"Ah. Yes. Good. Thank you … err … err …"

"Is there anything else you require, sir?" the Replacement asks.

"Yes. You can run these committee reports over to the Home Office. I shan't be needing them any more today."

"Certainly, sir. I shall do it at once." The Replacement picks up the reports and bows himself out.

"New clerk? What happened to whatsisname?" he hears the Honourable MP's companion remark as he leaves the room. He pauses on the threshold, to hear the Honourable MP's reply: "One goes, another comes. These clerks are all pretty interchangeable at the end of the day, aren't they?"

The Replacement's mouth forms a tight straight line. His thin fingers grasp the report folders compulsively, for the Honourable Thomas Langland, MP does not know about the relationship between the so-called 'interchangeable clerks' that he is so quick to dismiss. Langland has no idea that when a friend confides, over a drink, that he is sure his employer is 'up to something' and he is determined to get to the bottom of it if he can, and then mysteriously disappears a short while later, leaving no note to indicate where he has gone, it is the duty of the remaining friend to discover what he was hinting at.

That is precisely why the Replacement offered his services to this particular MP. It is his intention to keep his friend's seat warm, and his own ears and eyes open, so that when his friend reappears from wherever he has gone, he will be able to pass the desk back to him and hopefully enlighten him further as to what the MP they both currently serve is up to.

****

After another inadequate luncheon, Detective Inspector Stride returns to Scotland Yard, where he is summoned to the police mortuary. There have been, it appears, developments. The police surgeon's expression is almost seraphic as he greets him.

"Ah, detective inspector! Here you are at last. Good. And here," he gestures towards a shape lying on the slab and covered by a tarpaulin, "here, if I am not very much mistaken, is the body of our elusive man. Kindly brought in by Sergeant Foster and some bearers, all the way from Chalk Farm."

A tall saturnine man in a dark blue uniform with very shiny brass buttons is standing rigidly against the wall, his arms folded. He is staring at the tarpaulin with the apprehensive expression of somebody attending a waxwork exhibition without a catalogue. Stride gets out his handkerchief; the smell of spoiled meat and stagnant water is overwhelming, though he notices that Robertson seems to be impervious to it.

"Found floating in the Regent's Canal, under the cross-path bridge to Chalk Farm, sir," the sergeant says shortly. "One of the park keepers spotted it in the early hours of the morning. Poled it out with the help of a passing bargee."

Stride frowns. "In a canal? How come it wasn't discovered sooner?"

The sergeant grimaces. "It seems the body had been weighted down to stop it from surfacing. Only the weights weren't secured firmly enough and fell off, or maybe were struck off by a passing barge and the body came to the surface. We had read the notice you sent round about a stolen body, and as it seemed to fit the description, we decided to bring it here."

"I see."

"Perhaps you would like to view the actual body itself, detective inspector? I am sure you must be intrigued to see the corpse of a man who was spirited away in the night by persons unknown," Robertson says innocently, his hand poised over the tarpaulin, his eyes alight with mischief.

"If it is the same man," Stride demurs from behind his handkerchief. He does not move.

"Most assuredly it is. Your constable who originally discovered the body *in situ* has kindly identified it for me. So here we are. One corpse, delivered, stolen, disposed of in a canal, and now returned to us. The question one must ask is *cui bono*? ~ eh, detective inspector?"

Must one? Stride thinks grimly. The question foremost in his mind is whether he can leave before vomiting all over the floor.

"And I do not mean the common mistranslation and misconstruction of the Latin phrase as in 'to what good'," Robertson continues happily, rocking backwards and forwards on his heels. "No, indeed not. We have to go back to the original interpretation: *cui*, to whom; *bono*, is it for a benefit? That is, of course, beyond my remit as a humble surgeon though, so I shall leave it to your good self. Are you feeling quite alright, detective inspector, you look sightly green about the gills?" he remarks, noticing Stride's discomfort for the first time. "I must say, I have never understood how you solve murders if you can't stand the sight of dead people."

"I arrest live people," Stride mutters.

"I see. Well, perhaps that is something to be proud of. You will have my report on your desk as soon as I have performed my examination. Given the state of the body, I do not expect I shall be long. Good day to you, detective inspector."

He waves a dismissive hand and Stride departs with as much alacrity as he can muster. Once back outside in the fresh air, he feels his gorge heave. Stars dance in front of his eyes. Stride leans against a wall, breathing heavily while the world spins around him, which is where he is discovered a couple of minutes later by Jack Cully, who has stepped out to get a breath of air.

"Are you unwell? Shall I fetch some water?" he asks anxiously.

Stride raises his head. "No. I'll survive. It's just ~ that body, the smell ~ I don't know how Robertson can stand it. I couldn't do a job like that. Not in a million years."

Stride grimaces. He has never been good with dead bodies ~ beyond the point where he discovers them dead. His skill lies in working out the journey that they made to arrive at their final destination and then discovering who else was involved, and placing them in a police cell to await punishment. The two detectives return to the main building to await the police surgeon's findings. Nothing more is said, but both are inwardly hoping that the report, when it arrives on Stride's desk, will move the inquiry forward for, right now, there is so very little movement happening that it is almost static.

****

Meanwhile, over in the Chelsea house, Aunt Euphemia Harbinger has discovered that the small grey parrot, whose presence was initially viewed with suspicion, is actually proving to be highly entertaining. The bird is an excellent mimic. On its first day of occupation, it managed to terrify the maid by telling her to *'dust behind the sofa, lazy slut!'* in the exact intonation of her nephew Sherborne.

Bribed with sunflower seeds, the bird has provided her with a rich and enlightening window into the home life of Sherborne Harbinger, his wife and three children. The parrot has no social filter whatsoever: matrimonial altercations, juvenile squabbles and the comments of the Harbinger servants are all relayed in an endlessly fascinating and indiscreet stream of consciousness, punctuated by whistling and clicking its beak. One phrase, however, has been uttered more than any other, and so, the next time Sherborne and Hanover arrive, bearing flowers and obsequiousness, she asks, "Who is Harriet? The bird keeps asking for her."

"She is Hanover's sister; they are twins," Sherborne Harbinger says, reluctantly.

"I see. And why has she not been introduced to me?"

"I did not think she would be of any interest, dear aunt. She is of a rather wayward disposition, I am afraid, unlike Hanover, who is so devoted to you already. I decided an encounter with Harriet might be too much for you in your delicate state of health," he says, smoothly.

The old woman shoots him a sharp look. His dismissive comments are very much in line with what the parrot has already disclosed. "Isn't that for me to decide?" she says tartly. "Let her be brought to the house. The bird clearly misses her, and I should like to make her acquaintance."

Sherborne tries not to show his displeasure at the suggestion. But he has to acquiesce to the eccentric old woman's demands. There is too much inheritance riding on it. Thus, later that afternoon, arrayed in a frock that is slightly too tight under the arms, Harriet is shoved into the sitting room and introduced by her reluctant father. The parrot greets her arrival with wild enthusiasm. Aunt Euphemia, with interest.

"You may leave us now," she says, waving Harbinger away briskly. "Come back in an hour."

As soon as her nephew has gone, the old woman rings for refreshments, while Harriet and the parrot re-acquaint themselves with each other. Then, after Harriet has been furnished with a plate of biscuits and a glass of lemonade, she beckons her over to the sofa.

"Sit here, child. And tell me all about yourself," she says.

Obediently, Harriet places herself at the other end of the sofa. The two eye each other curiously. "So, Harriet, what would you like to be when you grow up?" the old woman asks.

"I think I should like to be a pirate chief," Harriet says. "Me and Polly would sail the Spanish Main, attacking Spanish galleons and stealing their treasure. I am writing a story all about pirates in my notebook."

The old woman is amused. "Oho! Is that so? I have never heard of a female pirate!"

Harriet leans in. "Have you not? Why, there was Madam Ching ~ she was a famous pirate chief who ruled the South China Seas. She had over a thousand ships under her command. Blackbeard only had four. I read all about her in a book."

"Indeed? And where would you live, pirate chief?"

"I'd have a beautiful house on a tropical island," Harriet tells her. "I'd have lots of dogs, and a pony. And I wouldn't get married, ever."

Aunt Euphemia eyes her thoughtfully. "I see. Well, you certainly know your own mind. But what's wrong with getting married?"

There is a pause. Harriet looks away, her face darkening. "Marriage means not being allowed to go anywhere alone. And getting shouted at when you say the wrong thing, so you run upstairs and cry in your bedroom when you think nobody hears you, but they do. They do hear."

The parrot bobs and ducks on its perch. Harriet bites her lip, takes a biscuit, breaks it into pieces, and starts feeding it to the bird. The old woman watches closely, her face a study.

Harriet continues. "If I couldn't be a pirate, then I should like to go to school. A proper school. I have read that there are proper schools, where girls can go and be educated, but I cannot go to one, father says, because Hanover and Timothy's education comes first, and education doesn't come cheap, so I must have a governess and learn sewing and globes, and how to order a dinner for when I get married."

Euphemia Harbinger feels a sudden surge of affection for the child ~ an emotion she has not experienced for many years. This young girl, with her hopes and dreams, her frank, fearless gaze, reminds her of somebody she had all but forgotten, for she, too, was once expected to be neither seen nor heard. Born in the middle of the French Revolution, when the whole of Europe was in turmoil, the youngest girl in a family that only cared about boys, she'd had to fight hard to obtain her liberty and fraternity ~ though she never achieved much equality.

Little is known of how Euphemia Harbinger acquired her jewels and money. Time and the disinclination of now defunct male Harbingers to talk about the family female 'black sheep' has obliterated the story of the beautiful young woman who, at sixteen, ran away from a stifling and oppressive home, who was fêted and loved by poets (Byron was one of her devotees), modelled for William Etty, and who spent a rackety and joyous life on the continent and in Brighton.

'Miss Phemy', as she was affectionately known to her inner circle, hosted a salon where writers, musicians and artists came to debate and perform. She was a successful gambler and was showered with expensive gifts by her many admirers. Given the choice, she would have happily remained below the family radar for the rest of her life but was eventually called back to London upon the death of her oldest brother, who left her the family home in his Will, having fallen out with all his own children.

From that day onwards, Euphemia Harbinger, unmarried, untethered from convention, has lived alone in the Chelsea house, watching as all the gay friends of her youth passed away, one by one. Now she is on the cusp of joining them. But there is time, she reminds herself every morning, when her eyes open upon a new day. The last thread has not been snipped. The vultures may be gathering, but the body still breathes.

The hour speeds by. Once the ice has been broken, the two find much to talk about. The old woman plies the girl with questions, which Harriet, unused to being listened to, delights in answering, her innocent comments confirming much that the old woman has suspected. All too soon however, Sherborne Harbinger appears in the doorway and indicates to Harriet that it is time to depart, as it is quite clear that she has tired her great aunt with her childish prattling.

Polite but warm farewells are said. The old woman indicates that another visit would be most welcome. Harriet agrees. Sherborne Harbingers smiles thinly and says that he is sure it could be arranged. The two adults know he is lying. Once father and daughter have quitted the Chelsea house to return to their hotel, the old lady rings the bell to summon her housekeeper.

"Bring me pen and paper, Rose," she commands, "I have important letters to write; there are matters I must look into. The child has piqued my interest. I want to find out about the state of girls' education and schooling in this country. I shall begin by writing to my Member of Parliament."

****

In a city of nearly three million inhabitants, you'd think the chances of casually running into somebody you know would be statistically remote. You'd be surprised how often it actually happens, though. For instance, here is Sherborne Harbinger, hurrying his daughter along the pavement, pushing his way through street vendors selling flowers, fruit, and themselves. And there, on the other side of the street, approaching in the opposite direction, is the music hall artist Micky Mokey, on his way back from a rehearsal.

Harbinger clutches his daughter's reluctant hand. Micky Mokey clutches the sheet music of a new song. He is humming the tune under his breath as he attempts to learn the words *('Oh Liza-Lou, I do love you, please love me true, be mine, all mine, dear Liza-Lou, please do')*. The song has been composed by the assistant stage-manager of the music hall, who wants it to be performed later tonight as a gift to his latest lady friend. She will be pointed out to Micky Mokey prior to his act, and he has been asked to get down on one knee at the end of the song and present her with a red rose.

The assistant stage-manager is confident that after this killing public gesture, she will succumb to his charms. Micky Mokey has no opinion one way or the other. So long as he gets paid. The rent is due and Little Azella's share is already in the pewter tankard on the mantelpiece. Micky Mokey has just reached verse 2 (same as verse 1 but with extra twiddly bits), when he hears a commotion from the opposite side of the street. Next minute, there is a screech of carriage wheels, the clatter of hooves, cursing, a loud neigh, and he looks round to spy a young girl standing in the middle of the road, screaming.

Without even thinking of the possible consequences of his actions, Micky Mokey leaps into the road, dodges round the traffic, scoops up the girl and carries her to his side of the pavement, where he sets her down. The girl immediately stretches her full length on the ground and starts drumming her heels. A crowd gathers. Micky Mokey is puzzled. The girl does not appear to have any superficial injuries. But something is clearly not right with her.

A second later, a smartly dressed, top-hatted man strides across the road, waving back the traffic with an imperious black gloved hand. He seizes the girl roughly by one arm and hauls her to her feet.

"For goodness' sake Harriet, you stupid, stupid child! What on earth were you thinking?" he exclaims. "You could have been killed!"

The crowd murmurs its agreement, then launches into its own tales of road accidents it has witnessed, fortuitous and fatal. The girl stares up at the man with an expression of deep loathing on her pale pointy face. Tears pour down her cheeks. Meanwhile Micky Mokey, having recognised the man instantly as the one he spotted in the music hall audience, attempts to filter his way to the outskirts of the crowd. No such luck.

"'Ere, gov'nor," a burly cloth-capped man says, taking the hapless music hall artist by the elbow and ordering the crowd to 'stand by and let us froo'. "Vis is ve man you should be thanking. Bloomin' hero, he is. Leaped out into ve road wiv not a thort for 'is own safety."

To loud applause (because who does not love a real hero?), Micky Mokey is propelled to the front of the crowd and deposited in front of Sherborne Harbinger (for it is he). The young man dips his hat over his eyes and stares down at his feet. But he need not have worried. When he eventually raises his head, there is not a flicker of recognition in Harbinger's face. Instead, he grasps Micky Mokey's hand, shakes it, and expresses his heartfelt gratitude.

Micky Mokey shrugs. The girl, who is now at the sniff-and-eye-wiping stage, regards him sullenly. Micky Mokey has the distinct feeling that she would have been quite happy to perish under the wheels of some passing cart. Harbinger reaches into his jacket pocket and pulls out a wallet. "Let me reward you, young man," he says.

Mickey Mokey shakes his head, but Harbinger will have none of it. Encouraged by the crowd, he hands some coins to the hero, who stuffs them reluctantly into his pocket. Harbinger continues. "Here is my card, young man. Please take it. I am currently staying with my family at the Excelsior Hotel. If you are ever passing, please give your name to the porter. My wife, I am sure, would like to thank you in person for rescuing our disobedient daughter." (He gives Harriet a violent shake.)

Mickey Mokey mumbles something vague and deprecating. Then he picks up his sheet music, now much trampled and dusty, and makes his way towards his lodgings. The crowd sees him off with another round of cheers and applause.

He didn't recognise me at all, he thinks amazedly. *I was a complete stranger to him*. As soon as he is clear of the scene, he digs into his pocket and retrieves the reward money he has been given. Lucky. Enough for a couple of weeks' rent and a few fish suppers on top. And no more than he deserves, he decides. Given the circumstances. All of the circumstances.

Less luckily, Harriet is frogmarched back to the hotel, where she is incarcerated in her room, with the instruction that she is to receive no supper. A family conference is then held in her parents' sitting room. It is attended by Hanover and the baby (who plays no part in the proceedings).

"She tried to run away," Sherborne tells his wife. "Would you believe it? I told you before we set out that we should have left her at home with the servants. She is nothing but a trial and a nuisance."

"But dear ..." his bosom companion begins.

"Had it not been for the quick actions of a passer-by," Harbinger continues, ignoring her interruption, "we might be paying out for a funeral. Wicked child! She has a perfectly nice home, she is fed and clothed, and STILL she isn't content with her lot. What more does she want?"

Hanover smirks. "She wants to be a pirate, Papa. She has told me often enough."

Sherborne rolls his eyes to the smoke-blackened ceiling. "Mad. Quite mad." He glares at his wife, who is sitting meekly in an armchair, her lace-mittened hands folded in her lap. "Does lunacy run in your side of the family, Charlotte? Because I can think of no other reason why Harriet has turned out the way she has. Two perfectly normal children, and this ... this chimera."

A chimera. Hanover mentally files the word away to use in a future argument with his sister. He doesn't know what it means, but it is clearly insulting. Hanover has a long list of such words. He likes to trot them out whenever (which is often) he and Harriet get into a scrap over something.

"Did she say why she wanted to run away, my dear?" Mrs Harbinger asks cautiously.

Her beloved snorts. "She said she desired to live on her own in future, like Great Aunt Euphemia ~ and there you have it." Sherborne starts pacing the room like a caged tiger. "This is why I didn't want to introduce her to the senile old fool. I knew, I just knew she'd pour some of her crazy ideas into Harriet's mind. Well, she won't be going back there again, and so I have told her. We can only hope aunt dies soon. It can't be much longer, surely. Her colour was very bad today."

"You don't think she told Harriet about ..."

Harbinger puts a warning finger to his lips. "Ahem. *Pas devant les infants*," he says in an execrable English accent.

Hanover pricks up his ears. This phrase always means something naughty is going to be talked about. Sherborne notices his son's sudden focused attention. "Go to your room Hanover, and dress for dinner," he orders. "The gong will be sounded in ten minutes."

Hanover drags slowly out of his parents' room. Passing his sister's door, he pauses, hearing muffled sobbing from within. He knocks loudly. "Pa says you ain't to have any dinner," he shouts through the keyhole.

"Don't want any."

"And he says you're a camera. So there!"

On the other side of the door, Harriet raises her head from the sieve of her cupped hands and frowns. What on earth? She sighs. Then, hearing her brother's footsteps retreating along the corridor, and his own door slamming shut, she goes to her bed and lifts the corner of the mattress. She takes out a brown-covered notebook, which she opens. The first page is entitled: 'The Adventures of a Pirate Queen'.

"Here you are, great aunt," she says, holding up the book to show to an invisible companion. "I've written the first big sea-battle. Would you like to hear it?" Harriet waits for a couple of seconds. Then she begins to read out loud to the empty room.

****

A few hours earlier, before these dramatic events take place, Miss Lucy Landseer, wearing her 'investigating bonnet' of yellow straw with green ribbons and carrying her work satchel, alights from an omnibus and walks the short distance to a pleasant, square, white-washed villa, where she is shown into a comfortable drawing room by a neat parlour maid.

Her client, Miss Rosalind Whitely is seated on a chintz sofa waiting for her to arrive. Tea is laid on a small rosewood table. She rises and greets her guest, thanking her for her attendance. Lucy settles herself in an armchair and glances covertly round the room, seeing if she can pick up any clues, while Rosalind Whitely pours tea into porcelain cups. Lucy adds two lumps of sugar to hers.

"Have you lived here long, Miss Whitely?" she asks politely, stirring the pale liquid vigorously.

"All my life, Miss Landseer. I was born here. I grew up here. This has always been my childhood home and I have never wanted to leave it."

"But you have never considered following a profession?" Lucy regards her thoughtfully.

"I did think some time ago about whether to train as a nurse. But then my father died, and Mama become so unwell that I abandoned any thoughts of it." Rosalind Whitely bites her lower lip.

Lucy gestures towards the mantelpiece. "That photograph is of your mother?"

"Indeed, Miss Landseer. I have a copy of it by my bed also. It was taken before she was stricken with her final illness."

Lucy rises and studies the picture. A sweet suffering face, the liniments of which can clearly be traced in the daughter.

"You say she died while you were away from the house. But presumably the servants were present. Have you spoken with them?"

"I have. The cook says she brought up Mama's supper as usual, but she was told to take it away as she had no appetite. My stepfather, Mr Brooke, was downstairs. He often works in his study until late. The housemaid says she came up to look in upon Mama before retiring herself, but was met on the landing by my stepfather, who told her Mama was sleeping peacefully and should not be disturbed. In the morning, the maid went to wake her, as usual, but ..." her voice trails away.

"I understand. So, the last person to see your mother alive was Mr Brooke."

"Yes. That is correct, Miss Landseer. A doctor was summoned at once and made an examination. It was his opinion that Mama had died peacefully in her sleep. Her heart had failed. She always suffered with a weak heart. He signed the death certificate on that basis."

Lucy makes a mental note. "It would aid me in my investigation if I might also have a photograph of your stepfather ~ perhaps there is one of him together with your mother that I could borrow?"

Rosalind Whitely stands. "There is the exact one you require upon my stepfather's desk in his study. If you care to follow me, Miss Landseer, I can supply you with what you request."

Lucy follows the young woman into what was the back parlour but is now clearly a 'man's room' with its smell of hair oil and cigars, shelves of books, a writing desk, and a comfortable armchair by the fireplace. Rosalind goes over to the mantelpiece. Then stops, frowning.

"Ah, I am sorry, it is no longer here."

Lucy indicates the writing desk. "Perhaps your stepfather couldn't bear to look upon what he has lost ~ may I?"

Rosalind nods, still frowning.

Lucy slides open the top drawer. Sure enough, there is a silver framed photograph placed face down. She extracts it, confirms that it is of the happy couple, and places it in her bag. Then, standing by the desk, she begins to casually play with the Cairngorm paperweight that is holding down a stack of documents.

"What occupation does your stepfather follow?" she inquires.

"I believe he works in an office somewhere in the West End, but do not ask me further, Miss Landseer. He always told my mother and I that the world of work was the man's domain, the home and hearth the woman's."

Did he indeed, Lucy thinks, drily.

Their conversation is suddenly interrupted by the maid, who informs Miss Whitely that the grocer's boy is at the door waiting for the order.

"Oh. I had forgotten that this is his day to call round. I must leave you for a short time, Miss Landseer," Rosalind says. "My stepfather is very particular about his meals. I shall return as quickly as I can."

"Please do not hurry back on my account," Lucy smiles seraphically. "I shall be quite content to study the room and make notes."

As soon as her client has left, Lucy picks up the top folder. She opens it to reveal a sheaf of documents. The top one appears to be a death certificate, signed and dated by a Doctor P. Q. Farris. She grabs her notebook and starts scribbling frantically. Hearing footsteps return, she hastily replaces the document in the folder and sets it under the paperweight once more.

"I am so sorry to leave you on your own, Miss Landseer," Rosalind Whitely says, entering the room.

Lucy demurs. Promising to return the photograph in due course, she takes her leave. Her visit has given her much to think about. Her client was quite right to seek her out, she thinks, as the omnibus jolts and rattles her back through the late afternoon traffic. Everything seems to be in perfect order, which must mean that there is something suspicious going on. Hopefully, she will soon be able to set her client's troubled mind at rest.

Back in her consulting room, Lucy takes the silver-framed photograph from her satchel and slides the cardboard retainer out of the back. To her surprise, she finds another photograph underneath. This one also depicts Mr Brooke, who is a good-looking man with luxurious side-whiskers and a moustache. He wears a black morning coat with top hat, and stands next to a plain-faced, stout, middle-aged woman, clad in a light dress and a pale bonnet with a lot of feathers. They are posing at the lych-gate of a church. On the back, someone has written: *Hitchin 1864*. She removes both photographs, placing them side by side on her desk.

Lucy reminds herself that, tempting though it may be, good detection work should never be based upon groundless speculation. She needs tangible proof that what she is looking at is what she suspects it is. She takes her copy of Bradshaw from the bookcase and consults it. There are regular trains leaving from London to Hitchin.

Tomorrow morning, bright and early, she will be on one of them.

****

Next morning, Detective Inspector Stride is reading the report from the police surgeon. Not out loud, but with a sufficient accompaniment of grunts and *sotto voce* muttering. The day is off to a slow start, scorching hot again. The window to Stride's office has been propped open with a ruler, but only seems to be admitting stale thrice-breathed air from the street below. A small drooping plant on the windowsill has considered its options and given up.

Stride reaches the last page of Robertson's analysis, slaps the report closed and looks across the desk at Jack Cully, who has been waiting patiently for him to reach the end.

"Translate it for me, Jack," Stride sighs.

"I think what Robertson is saying is that he is unable to make an accurate diagnosis due to the condition of the body, but while examining it, he has observed that the right eye is normal, whereas the left eye is fully dilated, which indicates the man suffered a blow to the head at some time. He therefore thinks, in the absence of any other indications, that this was the most likely cause of his death."

"See!" Stride exclaims. "Now I understand perfectly. So why can't he just say that, instead of presenting me with three pages of tetanic spasms, states of aggregation and some story about a Dr W. Ogle and his letter to the *Times* in August 1865, not to mention Xenophon and his retreating army who apparently suffered from eating honey collected from the Azalea plant. What is all that about? And how is it possibly relevant?"

"He does like to provide supporting evidence."

Stride huffs. "He enjoys showing off his knowledge is more like it."

"But his findings do confirm that the man was murdered, and with the theft of his body from the morgue, and then the attempted disposal in the canal, we have an unusual investigation, do we not?" Cully says. "How many bodies have been removed from Scotland Yard in our lifetime?"

Stride concurs. "Who is this man, Jack? What was so important about him? Why was he lured to some out of the way location? What did he do to deserve such a death?"

"I will put out an update on our last police appeal," Cully says. "It is no longer a case of 'Information is sought'. Now we have a confirmed murder on our hands. I think we should let some of the newspapers run the story as well. Maybe with an image of the man. It is imperative that somebody comes forward to tell us what they know.

"Meanwhile, I am going to visit Gold's Finest Cigar and Tobacco Emporium in the Strand. They stock these cigars, so I gather. I have had a letter from my own tobacconist, who promised to make some inquiries for me. I shall take young Constable Williams along with me and let him try his hand at questioning the proprietor. I think he has the potential to join the detective division, in time and with a steer in the right direction. As you are always saying, we need to bring on the youngsters."

Stride rolls his eyes and indicates that whatever the putative or future skills of the young constable, Cully is wasting his time running after a hare that does not exist. Or rather, the smoker of a cigar.

Cully goes to collect the young constable from the day room, where he is playing shove-halfpenny on a battered wooden board and together, they set off. The shop they seek is tucked back between Short & Co. Wine

Merchants, and the Strand Restaurant. Outside the door, a street advertiser, know colloquially as an 'animated sandwich' is alerting the passing public to the merits of *Phillips Teas: The Best and Cheapest* while being pestered by three bare-legged street Arabs who are capering around him and shouting, 'Oi mister, where's the mustard?'

Cully waves them aside. The two men go in, inhaling the rich smell of tobacco. The small shop is furnished with drums of snuff, carefully labelled, and long coils of tobacco, curled in three-foot lengths like black sausages, waiting to be sawn off and sold. There are boxes of cigars, snuff boxes galore, cigarettes, racks of pipes of all sizes and makes, leather pouches and matches. It is a sniffer and smoker's paradise.

The shop bell is answered by a small middle-aged man with a receding hairline and a droopy walrus moustache, stained with tobacco juice. He wears a dark suit that was made for somebody slightly bigger. His eyes bulge slightly when he sees that one of his potential customers is a uniformed constable.

"Oooh. Wasn't me officer," he squeaks, opening his eyes wide in faked innocence, "I didn't do it. Sweartogod."

Cully sighs. What is it about the mindset of some members of the general public that means they cannot resist having 'just a little joke' every time they encounter a police officer? Constable Williams turns to him for guidance.

"Mr Gold, is it?" Cully says, smoothly. "I am sure you are not guilty, sir. Of whatever it was you didn't do. However, we are not here about that. We are from Scotland Yard's detective division, making some inquiries in the area. We'd very much appreciate it if you could confirm whether you supply a certain brand of cigar." Cully places the gold cigar band onto the counter. "This brand of cigar, if you'd be so kind."

The shop owner stares at the band. Then he glances from one man to the other. Finally, he addresses himself to Constable Williams. "Detectors, are you? Never met any detectors before. On a case, then?"

Constable Williams nods.

"Is it serious? How serious? Murder? Would it be murder?"

Constable Williams is just about to reply when Cully intervenes. This is the primal error of first-time investigators, he thinks wearily, a tendency to answer questions rather than ask them.

"The cigars, sir?" he prompts.

The tobacconist picks up the cigar band and studies it. "Yes, I stock these. Just a few boxes, mind. You're talking about a very nice but very expensive smoke, gents. These cigars are hand rolled by experts using only the finest picked leaves. Each one is a little masterpiece. Not for the everyday smoker. Oh no, not for them, indeed."

"Can you give us a list of customers who purchase them?" Cully asks, getting out his notebook.

"Ah. Well. Now. That's a question, isn't it?" the tobacconist says. "I'm afraid I couldn't possibly tell you that, gents. Secrets of the smokers' confessional, as it were. I can tell you that they are enjoyed by the sort of gentlemen who send their servants to buy them. Which in itself says something, doesn't it? I don't think people of that class would be involved in anything criminal, would they? And it's more than my job's worth to give you their names."

Cully pulls a face. It is clear this line of inquiry is not going to produce any fruit. "Many thanks, Mr Gold. You have been most helpful," he lies. "Come constable, we shall not detain this good man any longer."

The look of disappointment upon the tobacconist's face is almost comical. "That's it? That's all? But what about the murder? Aren't you going to tell me about it?"

"Murder? I don't recall saying anything about a murder, sir," Cully says. "Nor did my officer say anything about murder, as I recall. We are merely inquiring about a brand of cigars. I would advise you not to let your imagination run away with you. Many a decent individual has found himself in very hot water indeed from having an over-active imagination. Sir."

He bestows upon the luckless tobacconist a smile so wooden it could have served as an ironing-board. "And now, having pursued our inquiries, we shall be on our way," he continues, ushering his youthful companion swiftly out of the street door.

"Never reveal your intentions, Tom," he tells the crestfallen young officer. "Nor allow yourself to be diverted. And do not give anybody the slightest hint of what you are investigating, because they will immediately put two and two together and make five. Which will then become six or seven, which will then leak into the public domain like spilt treacle and upset Detective Inspector Stride. In my experience, a rumour can spread faster than the truth, and that can be fatal for the success of an investigation."

"Yes, Mr Cully. Sorry, sir."

Cully pats him on the back. "Cheer up, young Tom. You have a long road ahead of you, but you are making good progress. I see a food stall up ahead. How about something to eat and drink before we go back to the Yard? My treat. Would a ham sandwich and a cup of coffee suit?"

Constable Williams indicates that it would suit very well. So Cully steers his newest recruit in the direction of some street sustenance. In his experience, young constables have a voracious appetite. Besides, they have some serious thinking to do on their return to Scotland Yard, which is always better done on a full stomach.

****

Miss Lucy Landseer, on the other hand, is a long way from eating and drinking, having consumed a very early breakfast before making her way to Kings Cross station to catch a train to the small market town of Hitchin. Now, as the train pulls into the station, she is also a long way from London. Lucy alights, asks for directions from one of the porters, then sets off towards the town centre.

She is on a quest to find the church whose lych-gate features on the photograph she discovered secreted underneath that of her client's stepfather and mother. In the end, it is an even easier quest than she'd thought: the first person she shows the photograph to, directs her straight there. Lucy, a child of the manse herself, knows the form: the vicarage will be the nearest house, slightly shabby, probably in need of a lick of paint and with a straggling unkempt garden, situated in close proximity to an immaculately kept graveyard. The church, in her experience, reveres the dead far more than the living.

Sure enough, it is exactly as she pictured it. Lucy scuffs up the dusty vicarage path and knocks on the paint-peeling door, which is opened by a very young girl in a grubby pinafore trailing a skipping rope. She eyes her curiously. Lucy identifies her provenance, so bends down and asks gently if Papa is at home and if so, might she speak with him about a family matter of some urgency?

The request (well, it is a family matter ~ just not her family) succeeds, and a few minutes later, she is sitting in the kindly-faced vicar's study, a high-ceiling book-lined room, cold even though there is a heatwave outside, explaining earnestly and not entirely truthfully that she has come to find her aunt, her only living relative, whom she believes might dwell hereabouts because, look, she has a picture of her and it shows the gate of the church, does it not?

The vicar studies the photograph carefully, while Lucy smiles and mentally crosses her fingers. Then he nods. "Yes, indeed, I recall marrying this couple. Beatrice Shipper and Francis Brooke. She was the owner of the confectioner's shop in the high street ~ you probably passed it on your way here. Her sponge cakes and gingerbread were known throughout the town for their excellence."

"Was?" Lucy queries.

"I'm afraid she died a year or so after the marriage. Heart failure, I seem to remember. Such a loss to the town. The shop is rented out to a new baker, but it isn't the same. Not at all. I am so sorry to be the bearer of bad news. Have you come far?"

"Yes," Lucy tells him, deciding that geographically, London probably fits into the 'far' category. "Oh, I didn't know Aunt Beatrice had died. Nobody wrote to me. Oh, how very sad." She wrings her hands in a tragic manner. "I wonder, would it be too much to view the parish records of her marriage. At least I could see her signature, and that would be something to take away with me," she asks.

Lucy sighs deeply, clasping her hands in her lap and casting her eyes down to the wooden boards of the floor. It has been said of Lucy Landseer by those who knew her, that the stage lost a potentially shining star when she decided to enter the literary profession.

Who could resist such a plea? Certainly not a man of the cloth, for whom kindness and charity are part of the genetic makeup. Lucy is escorted across to the church. A big leather-bound ledger is brought from the back and placed on the wooden eagle lectern, and after a short interval of page turning, the book is folded back at the relevant page. She scans the details, although it is only the man, not the woman who interests her. She reads:

Name and Surname: Francis Brooke, *Age*: 42, *Condition*: Widower, *Rank or Profession*: Businessman, *Residence at the time of Marriage*: 51 Borough High Street, London.

Lucy feels an electric shock go through her. '*Widower*'? What is this? She had guessed from the second photograph, that Rosalind's stepfather had been married before he met and married Rosalind's mother. But twice? This is not what she is expecting at all. Carefully keeping her face neutral, she thanks the vicar, agrees she would like to see her aunt's final resting place, and follows him out to the quiet churchyard, where, after spending a suitable amount of time in thoughtful contemplation of the very plain headstone, she announces that she must return to London.

"I am so sorry your journey has been in vain, Miss Landseer," the vicar says. "I have been racking my brains for something that might make it worthwhile. I wonder, now, if you have the time, you might pay a call upon Miss Clarissa Cameron ~ she and your aunt were neighbours and good friends, I believe. She only lives a step from the church, and I am sure she'd welcome you, and possibly be able to tell you a little more about your aunt's life. Shall I write a short note of introduction?"

Lucy's eyes sparkle and she quickly agrees. The note is speedily composed and handed over, and soon, Lucy stands outside a black painted door with a shiny lion's head knocker. Pink and white striped old English roses twine round the windows, gently scenting the air with their sweet perfume, and a blackbird fusses in the beech hedge that surrounds the house.

The door opens. The note is handed to the servant-girl, who bears it into the house, returning in a few seconds to say that her mistress is at home and can receive her. Lucy steps into a white-painted parlour with black wooden ceiling beams. She notes the good, dark oak furniture, blue and white jugs on the mantelpiece and bright polished brass fire irons. This is the home of a comfortably well-off country gentlewoman.

The mistress of the house, dressed in an old-fashioned sprigged muslin dress, her grey hair tucked neatly into a frilled day cap, rises from the chair where she is engaged in some complicated crochet work, and greets her unexpected visitor politely. Lucy is placed in the opposite chair and invited to explain her visit. Which she does. When she has finished explaining, Mrs Cameron nods thoughtfully at her a couple of times.

"I am sorry you have come so far on a wasted errand, my dear. Yes, Beatrice and I were neighbours for several years. She inherited the house next door from her parents. There was a younger brother, but I gather he went to the bad and left the country, and they never heard from him again. Would he be your family connection?"

Lucy assumes an expression of incredible innocence and does not respond.

"Ah well, we can choose our friends, but we can't choose our family, can we," Mrs Cameron continues. "So, here you are, ready to make reparations, but you have come too late."

"I know that now. What can you tell me about my relative, and her marriage? Was it not unexpected?"

Mrs Cameron looks down, fiddling with her crotchet hook. "It is not for me to say, Miss Landseer. Beatrice lived with her parents ~ her father was a master baker until they died. She helped in the shop and nursed them both devotedly until the end of their lives. She then took over the reins of the shop. She was rather abrupt in her manner, and perhaps not as pleasant in her disposition as other women in the town, and so did not attract many suitors. She also suffered with her legs and was eventually recommended the water cure at Tunbridge. She met Mr Brooke, her future husband, while being treated there, and married him in the local church."

"It was a happy marriage?"

"It seemed so. I never heard any quarrels. Then her old trouble returned, and her husband took her up to London to see a specialist. And there she died. It was her final wish to be brought back to Hitchin and be buried in the local churchyard, next to her parents, in the town where she was born."

Lucy sits silently, taking this information on board. "And the house next door?"

"It was sold. A couple from Royston and their children live there now."

Lucy waits to see if anything else is going to be imparted. When it is not, and the woman picks up her crochet hook once more in a pointed manner, she takes the hint, thanks her hostess profusely for sparing her the time, and departs.

On the way back to the station, Lucy Landseer calls in at the baker and confectioner's, superficially to buy a nice cake for the homeward journey. In the course of conversation, she finds out that the shop and the living quarters above are rented by the baker, and the landlord lives in London town.

A good day's work, Lucy decides, as the train chugs through the Hertfordshire countryside towards London. She has learned much today, none of it to Mr Brooke's credit. She munches her cake and contemplates her next move. She has never strayed south of the river before. Now it looks as if she is about to make her first foray into the territorial unknown. And who knows what she is going to discover when she gets there?

****

There is not much to discover about the Honourable Thomas Langland that isn't blatantly apparent to all his fellow MPs: he is cunning, ruthless and with absolutely no scruples. Ideal qualifications for a Member of Parliament. Equally ideal for the various other pies into which he has inserted a finger, the pie in this present case being his ownership of a racehorse called Spartacus, stabled on his country estate in Suffolk.

For the provenance of Spartacus, you have only to turn to the pages of *The General Stud Book*, where his pedigree is laid out for all to view. His dam was one of the foals bred directly from the Godolphin Arabian, the stallion sold by Louis XV and subsequently brought to Britain to improve the native stock. The horse is a noble animal, a bay with a white star on his forehead. He is bred to run and to win. Currently, he has done exactly that, and a lot of guineas have deposited themselves in Langland's bank account.

Here is Thomas Langland now, travelling alone in a first-class carriage. It is Thursday night, and the House has risen early, affording him the opportunity to catch the afternoon train to his Suffolk mansion.

London, in the heat of a sweltering summer such as this, carries little appeal for a man like Langland. The Season is drawing to its exhausting close, and he has preparations to make for the upcoming shooting and hunting that will follow in the autumn. Parliament is about to go into recess, after which he will host a number of lavish 'Friday to Monday' entertainments in the run-up to Christmas.

Langland's wife, as befits the consort of an up-and-coming MP, has remained on the family estate, supervising the staff, preparing for his return and overseeing the upbringing of several small Langlands, whose names he sometimes confuses. Like the horse, she also comes from good pedigree breeding stock, although unlike the horse, she has no Arabian lineage.

As the train puffs out of London, Langland settles back with his copy of *The General Stud Book*. After perusing the page featuring Spartacus, he turns to other pages, where various thoroughbred mares are listed. He takes out a pen, and circles a couple, noting their proximity to his own stables.

His horse is now mature enough to consider his stud potential. Langland has heard on the racing grapevine that the owner of Liberty Hall, descended from the Darley Arabian, made £50,000 in stud fees alone. Then there is the money to be made from any offspring, should they develop the qualities of a good flat-racer.

Of course, Langland is not prepared to fork out vast amounts from his private income. That is not how it's done. He will form a syndicate: he provides the horseflesh, other men put in the amount needed to buy a top-quality pedigree mare, or two. The profit will derive from the sale of the offspring, and any stud fees on top. He has a list of potential marks, most of whom are racing afficionados already. It should be easy to get them to come up with the money.

Of course, the owners of the mares he has selected might not want to part with them or might demand more than Langland is prepared to pay. But there is a way round that, too. As a local landowner, Langland is privy to all the land disputes, boundary issues, tenancies, business quarrels and sundry other major or petty rivalries that plague his constituents. His agent keeps him up to date. Also, as an MP he is expert in wheedling, requesting, ordering, commanding, cajoling and if that fails to achieve its objective, in forcing, bullying, intimidating, threatening, and making his opponents' lives pretty miserable.

He is therefore almost certain that the owner of Iris, the mare he has decided to purchase, will be amenable to parting with her once the position of his eldest son, his overdue rent and his lease has been made quite clear to him. Yes, there is always a way round any problem, Langland reflects, as he pockets the stud book, and turns his attention to a copy of the *Sporting Times*. *Oderint dum metuant:* let them hate me as long as they fear me. Langland attended Eton, so he is fond of the classical Roman emperors, especially Caligula.

The train pulls into his station and Langland alights. His coachman is waiting for him, ready to drive him the short distance to the Georgian mansion, set in its own extensive grounds. It was the family home of his wife but has now passed to him upon the death of Lord Fortescue-Arbuthnot, his father-in-law. As soon as they pull up in front of the house, Langland heads straight for the stable where his groom is busy oiling Spartacus' hooves. Langland greets the man, then leans on the lower stable door, watching him working while at the same time devouring the horse with greedy eyes.

Spartacus won at Sandown Park, came second at Ascot, won again at Goodwood and again at Epsom in June. The animal has the stamina of ten horses, he reflects. He will run him in September at Haydock Park and November at Cheltenham. Meanwhile, a time of rest, short gallops and good nutrition is required to prepare him for the autumn season. The horse needs to be in tip-top condition. Langland can almost hear the chink of guineas. He spends some time talking over his future plans with the groom. After an hour or so, he reluctantly tears himself away and goes into the house to say hello to his wife and assorted offspring.

****

Detective Inspector Stride is a man of his word. Or rather, of many words. His grasp of the English vernacular and his ability to employ it is both widely known and admired amongst his colleagues. Groups of them have been known to gather outside his office just to listen to him expostulating on some matter that has displeased him. As is the case right now.

The day had started so well. Stride's noisy neighbours had taken their quarrelsome marriage and screaming offspring to Margate, affording him a decent night's sleep. His favourite coffee-stall holders were back to provide him with the noxious black brew that fuelled his thinking processes. Only the weather was still working against him, but he was prepared to give it the benefit of the doubt as he strode into Scotland Yard and headed for his office, where the reports of the previous night, plus the newspapers of the current day awaited his attention.

At which point, Stride's ability for explosive expletives erupted. With such force that a couple of passing constables paused outside his door. The word got round, and soon they were joined by a couple more, so that by the time Jack Cully appears on the scene, the corridor outside Stride's office is packed. Some of the officers are diligently making notes for future use.

Cully elbows his way through, and, to a muttered chorus of disappointment, enters the office. Cautiously. "Everything alright in here?" he inquires, innocently.

In response, Stride waves a furious hand at a copy of *The Inquirer*. "I knew he'd do it! The swine! The pusillanimous penny-a-liner petty little hack! Look at this, Jack and give me one good reason why I shouldn't go straight round to Fleet Street and demand his head?"

Cully picks up the offending newspaper. The banner headline on the front-page reads: **Lost Body of Murdered Man MYSTERIOUSLY Returned! Who**

Is Scotland Yard in League With? He reads on. The piece focuses on the long-defunct crime of bodysnatching. There are oblique references to Burke and Hare, and lurid details of what happens in medical dissections. It is the sort of piece guaranteed to make readers either very angry, or very queasy.

"Ah," Cully says, replacing the journal upon Stride's desk. "Oh dear. How unfortunate. I fear this will be taken at face value, won't it?"

"Of course it will! This is exactly the purpose! He wants people to think we are criminals, supplying London hospitals with bodies by the back door. Journalists like Dandy are utter scum. I only hope one day they will vanish off the face of the earth, and take their false stories with them," Stride exclaims, sitting himself back down.

"Have any of the other newspapers taken the same line?"

Stride parcels out the pile of daily papers. "See for yourself. I didn't get any further than *The Inquirer.*"

Cully pages rapidly through *The London Express*, *The Telegraph*, *The Times* and *The Illustrated London Gazette*. No references to bodysnatching.

"It looks as if the rest of the press have stuck to the information we supplied," he says. "Including the police artist's drawing we sent to them. So hopefully someone will now come forward."

"Oh, I am quite sure they will," Stride remarks grimly. "Expect a crowd of irate citizens demanding to know whether their deceased relative was passed to a local hospital for medical investigation before being released for burial ~ yes, I know it is illogical but that is how their minds will work. No smoke without fire. There will be questions asked in Parliament, no doubt, and a sharp letter from the Home Secretary."

Cully is used to Stride's tendency always to assume the worst outcomes, so he merely nods in an agreeing fashion without saying he actually agrees with him. At which point there is a knock at the door, which opens to reveal a day constable.

"Desk sergeant says: can you come to the foyer, sir. There's some people complaining that their son's body felt 'light' when it was returned to them, and they want to find out if anything was 'taken' during the autopsy."

Stride gives Cully a despairing look. "See? Just as I told you. And so it begins."

****

The Replacement bends his head over his work. His pen moves swiftly along an imaginary line. He tries not to show the intensity of his emotion. This MP, this rich, over-privileged human being exists in a bubble. He has no idea what it is like to be poor, to be homeless, to see your children crying for food and know you have not the wherewithal to feed them.

Every day of his working life the Replacement encounters such people as he walks to and from his place of employment. He sees toothless old women sitting in doorways, minding rag-wrapped infants for farthings. Young boys turn bare-footed cartwheels for pennies. Housewives in crumpled aprons and tattered shawls queue outside small grocers' shops for the stale loaves, reduced at the end of the day. The only places to prosper are pawnbrokers, and gin-palaces.

Part of his frustration with his employer, apart from his inability to recall his name, lies in his own lack of progress in working out what part, if any, the Honourable Thomas Langland, MP played in the sudden absence of his friend. The Replacement is sure the answer might lie in the locked drawer in Langland's office. If he could only have sufficient time, and some suitable implement, he might open the drawer and ascertain for himself.

But even though the MP he serves indulges in long lunches, and is in the House to speak or on a committee most afternoons, the Replacement does not dare effect a break-in. Other clerks run in and out of his room with memoranda or reports or messages from other ministries. Langland has, on occasions, returned unexpectedly, forcing his clerk to invent some fictitious reason why he has left his place and entered the inner sanctum of his employer.

The Replacement's pen scratches on. Meanwhile, Langland, back from a weekend at his country house, is in an unusually talkative mood today. He stands in the doorway, arms folded while he describes the racehorse he owns, and his plans for the next season. He speaks as if talking to some equinely ignorant person, using technical words, expecting his clerk to be impressed. The Replacement remembers the heat of the brazier, the hiss of the shoes as they were thrust into a pail of water, the tap-tap of his father's hammer, the soft whistling sound he made to keep the horses calm while their new shoes were fitted.

He doubts if his employer has ever curry-combed a horse's mane, or picked stones out of its hooves, or run his hand down its velvet neck. The care of his horse is of no account. He has grooms to do that. It is only about what the animal is worth. About money. About winning. And once the fine animal has served his purpose, he will be sold to some knacker's yard and boiled down for glue.

When the bells of the city ring out the mid-day, the Replacement slides off his high stool and leaves the office for a breath of un-fresh air and a ham sandwich. He joins the stream of city clerks also seeking refreshment at the numerous pubs, coffee houses and small eateries that crowd the streets and alleyways around Westminster, losing himself amidst the restless and noisy activity.

There are two types of clerks: the spruce young ones, dapper in bright boots, tight coats, well tied cravats and splendidly coloured waistcoats, who work at the Admiralty or Somerset House, and the solicitors' clerks, soberly clad in black, with white cravats and waistcoats who mill around Parliament Street and Palace Yard, complete with blue and crimson bags.

The Replacement fits into neither category. He is no cynosure of fashion, nor does he have the gravitas and training of a legal clerk. He has merely been plucked from a pool of similar nonentities to fill another man's boots. Temporarily, he hopes. Indeed, his status is so insignificant that his employer still cannot remember his name.

He enters a small, neglected tavern, frequented by those who cannot afford to spend much on their mid-day meal, and slides into a vacant booth. Spilled ale and breadcrumbs adorn the table, signs of the previous occupant and negligent bar staff. The Replacement picks up a much-thumbed copy of the morning paper and engrosses himself in it while he waits for his order to be taken.

As he idly flicks through descriptions of the antics of the upper classes, advertisements for goods landed, and the usual strange summer stories about talking goldfish, his eye is caught by the headline halfway down page five: **Mystery of A Murdered Man** ~ intrigued, he begins to read the article.

A few minutes later, the Replacement hurries out of the tavern, lunchless, the newspaper folded and poking out of his coat pocket. He glances swiftly left, then right, after which he darts across the road and sets off in the direction of Scotland Yard.

Arriving at the police office desk, the Replacement shows the story to the constable on duty, explains why he has come, and is directed to the Anxious Bench to await the return of one of the two detectives dealing with the investigation.

A short but interesting time elapses. The Replacement shares the bench with a large indignant woman smelling of onions, who, spotting a captive audience, proceeds to tell him all about 'her Samuvell wot was a wictim of a crool gang of dockside robbers' but whose body had been 'meddled wiv' by the forces of law and order and she was here to get justice for him, she was and she wasn't going to stir from this spot until she did.

The Replacement hasn't a clue what she is talking about, but he recognises her as one of the populace who conduct their daily lives under the tyranny of the rich and powerful, and is therefore a kindred spirit, so he resorts to nodding sympathetically while making suitably shocked noises, such that when Detective Sergeant Jack Cully enters, and is directed to where he is sitting, the woman is most reluctant to part from him, having discovered a sympathetic soul.

Cully introduces himself, asks what he can do to help the pale young man, who sits so upright, his hands clasped between his knees, his expression tense. The Replacement indicates that it is a matter to be discussed in private. Cully invites him to rise and follow him. Once seated in the small stuffy office Cully shares with two other detectives, the Replacement produces the newspaper and folds it back to the article.

"I believe I may be able to identify the man in this newspaper story," he says, hesitantly. "It is possible that he used to be a clerk in the same parliamentary office where I now work. I cannot be absolutely certain ~ but from the description in the newspaper, I think it could be him. Do you have a list of his clothes and personal items? He was a friend of mine and I could probably identify him from those."

"Ah. I see. Unfortunately, he has been buried," Cully says. "In this heat, we couldn't keep the body for long, I'm sure you understand. But I certainly have the list of the clothes he wore and there is a box of his personal possessions. If you can tell us who he was, I should be most grateful as we would then be able to let his family know. I shall fetch the list for you."

Cully is gone a few minutes, giving the Replacement time to get control of his feelings and prepare himself. Even so, when he studies the list, recognises the clothes, sees the watch chain, black pen, and other possessions that he has seen about the person of his friend on so many occasions, he feels his throat clotting, and hot tears fill his eyes.

Suddenly, he is faced with the truth; he had always secretly hoped that somewhere, his friend still lived and he would meet him again one day when they would share a drink and exchange stories, and he would tell him everything he'd discovered about Thomas Langland during his absence. In his short life, the Replacement has only ever counted two men as friends. One emigrated to America to seek a better world. The other now lies under the sod in an unmarked grave.

Cully observes his pain. He waits until control has been achieved, then pushes a piece of paper across the desk. "Can you give us the name of your friend, his address, and his place of work?"

The Replacement writes. After a few minutes, he raises his head. "Where was his body found? I should like to visit the place. To get a picture in my mind of his last moments. And I should like to know where he was buried also."

Cully jots down the locations of both. "I can also give you the name of the constable who discovered the body. He will be able to answer any further questions you might have. For now, please accept my condolences and know that I and my colleagues are grateful to you for coming forward. Your information will be of much help in finding his family."

The Replacement nods. He sits in silence for a few seconds. Then he rises, shakes Cully's hand without making any eye contact, and departs, clutching the scrap of paper. Cully waits until the sense of sadness has evaporated from the room. Then he goes to find Stride and convey the good news.

Detective Inspector Stride listens attentively as Cully outlines the interview with the young parliamentary clerk. "So now at last we have a name for our victim," he says. "Good. We are making progress. I dislike having to bury a man without his next of kin knowing that he died."

"You don't think that his employer could have had anything to do with the death?" Cully muses. "I wonder whether the cigar we found could have some connection to him? A rich man's cigar?"

Stride glances down at the Replacement's note and pulls a face. "The Honourable Thomas Langland, MP? Much as I dislike members of Parliament, especially members of the Conservative Party, I doubt it. Too risky. In this day and age, it is almost impossible for a man in high office to keep his private affairs out of the public eye. There's always some journalist with a notebook standing in the shadows ready to expose him. And once his dark deeds hit the front page, that's the end of him."

"So why was the man murdered? It clearly wasn't for his possessions."

Stride shakes his head. "Who knows? Why does anyone murder? Usually, in my experience, it comes down to either money or passion. In this case ~ we may never know. The young man you spoke to did not mention a significant relationship? No? Well then. I am as in the dark as you."

"I still don't understand why the theft of the body."

"A rather crude attempt by whoever committed the deed to prevent the finger of blame pointing at him?"

Cully purses his lips. "Seems rather desperate. I still think it might be worth speaking to Mr Langland before we close the investigation. Just to confirm that he had nothing to do with it. Do you agree?"

Stride picks up a pencil and starts twirling it thoughtfully between his fingers. "Ah. Well, Jack, we'd have to proceed very carefully if we decide to go down that path. Yes, indeed we would. The man's a popular member of Parliament. He delivers speeches that get recorded in the papers. He sits on various influential committees. There is talk of making him a Cabinet Minster someday soon.

"If we start making waves, trying to incriminate him in anything as sordid as a murder, even if he has nothing to do with it, next thing we know, there'll be a letter of complaint put in to the Home Secretary, and then we'll have all and sundry breathing down our necks. Let alone the popular press. I can just imagine the headlines in *The Inquirer: 'Popular Politician Persecuted by Police.'*"

A price worth paying, Cully thinks, though he does not share his thoughts. "But the cigar ..." he begins.

Stride cuts across him. "Ah, yes, the curious incident of the cigar in the night-time. Was the cigar smoked in the night-time? Or was it dropped there, accidentally, by some passing smoker? We will never know. And we have no way of finding out. The cigar, to mix metaphors, is rather a red herring."

"So where do we go from here?" Cully asks.

"We do not go anywhere," Stride says. "We write to his family. If they wish us to pursue matters, then we may have to continue. Until then, as far as I am concerned, the investigation is closed. We have gone as far as we can."

But have we? Cully muses, as he makes his way back to his desk. Why did someone go to a lot of trouble to break into the police morgue, steal a body, and then dispose of it in the canal? And what did this young man know that made his death and subsequent disappearance a matter of such importance?

****

Meanwhile, the Replacement hurries back to his place of work. He is still in shock at the revelation of his friend's murder. As he walks, he thinks about the interview with the detective. Should he have mentioned his friend's suspicions? Ought he to return and reveal what was told to him in confidence? What difference might it make? If any.

He hears a church bell strike the three-quarters, which means he has exceeded the time allocated for his luncheon. Another time, then. He picks up the pace, but as it happens he is in luck, for Langland himself has not returned. The House is on its last few days before recess, and a certain laxity is therefore now permissible. Not for the clerks, of course, who will be expected to labour on over the summer.

The Replacement takes the cover off his desk, sets up his pens and inks and begins to copy some papers, but his thoughts are adrift. This was where his friend sat. This his desk, every groove and scratch in the wooden surface was familiar to him. Here he sat on the day he met his death. What thoughts were going through his mind, as his pen flowed smoothly across the paper?

Did he think of the evening meeting they were both due to attend? The Replacement casts his mind back to the room above the Star & Garter public house, the German speaker, his black beard, and tweed suit stained with tobacco, his crumpled cream shirt and untidy cravat, the eager audience of young men hanging on his every word as he expounded upon philosophy and German literature.

The Replacement had sat at the back, letting the words flow over him, his eyes periodically straying to the door, wondering where his friend was, why he hadn't sent word that he couldn't be there. After the lecture, he had gone straight round to his friend's lodgings, only to be told by the landlady that a message had been delivered and her lodger had gone out to meet someone. He had not returned. He had not returned the next night either.

And then, a request went out for a new clerk, and the Replacement was plucked from the pool and selected to take over his desk. This desk. It was just as if his friend had evaporated, had never existed. He had not made a specific link between the actual disappearance and the man whose office lies just a few steps beyond the oak door. A coincidence. But now, now he has discovered that his friend has been murdered, his thoughts are beginning to move along that path, although he cannot see any clear connection at present.

Time passes. The light thins. The day wears on. His friend's presence is here in the room, insisting on being acknowledged. He finishes copying another report. He sets down his pen. He raises his head. Listens. No familiar footsteps on the stair. He checks the time: if he hasn't appeared by now, it is unlikely that the Honourable Thomas Langland is going to put in an appearance today.

The Replacement packs away his writing materials and covers his desk. He is tired, so tired he can feel it in his bones. But it is time to begin his journey to that place where his only friend drew his final breath, in the hope that he can make that connection, to help him discover what happened on that fateful night. He steps out of the room and begins to walk.

It takes him some time to find the building site and when he finally does, it is to see the workmen packing up for the day. The Replacement stands on the other side of what was once a small street but is now the muddy access road to a cluster of brand-new cheap houses, sprouting like fungi out of the London clay.

A large sign affixed to a hoarding proclaims: **Wm. Boxworth & Co. Fine New Dwellings for Sale or Rent. Inquire at the Site Office.** Some half-demolished buildings still remain, overlooking the site, with their side walls already taken down. Sprigged wallpaper and paint, wooden floorboards, a dresser, bear witness to previous occupants now scattered to the four winds, or probably a couple of already over-crowded tenements close by.

The Replacement is not sure exactly where his friend met his end. He walks up and down past the wooden hoardings, trying to summon him mentally. As he reaches the corner of one side, he is hailed roughly.

"Oi, you, young man ~ what're you doing here?"

He turns. The interlocuter is a small squat man in a loud check suit. He has dusty work-boots, small suspicious eyes, and an ugly pock-marked face. He carries a set of keys and a folder of documents. The Replacement presumes he is the site foreman. He approaches.

"Please excuse my presence. A good friend died close to this site. I came to see for myself. That is the whole purpose of my visit. I mean no harm."

The small ugly man comes closer. And closer still. He stares hard at the Replacement. There is no warmth or compassion in the stare; it is the sort of stare a vulture might bestow on potential prey. The Replacement holds his position. He isn't committing any crime, he tells himself. The man has no weapon, and there are plenty of workmen streaming out of the gate, so he is not in any danger.

"I see," the man says slowly, never taking his eyes off the young man's face. "And 'oo was this friend of yours, if you don't mind me asking?"

Something about the tone of the question, coupled with the stare, that is going on for far too long for comfort, starts warning bells sounding in the Replacement's brain. A feeling of repulsion and of something akin to fear begins to steal over him.

"Oh, he was someone who went to a discussion group I attended. I did not know where he had actually died until I read an article about it in the newspaper," he says vaguely.

"Oh, did you now. Read it in the newspaper, eh? And what did this h'article say?"

"It had a description of him and a request from the police for help in identifying who he was."

"Which, as a good citizen, you went and did, I presume?"

The Replacement nods. The way the man is studying him so intently is unsettling him. He feels an urgent need to remove himself from his presence. "I shall go now," he says. "I apologise for disturbing you."

"Wait up, wait up, young 'un," the man says, swinging his bunch of keys in what could be interpreted as a threatening manner. "Tell me some more about this friend of yours. What was his name? Where did he work?"

"We were friends, that is all. Good day to you, sir," the Replacement says, walking away. His heart is pounding. When he has put some distance between himself and the building site, he stops and glances back: the man hasn't moved. He is still standing there, staring fixedly after him, swinging his keys slowly in one hand.

****

Miss Lucy Landseer, female private detective, is also trying to make connections in her ongoing investigation into the life and wives of Francis Brooke. Here she is crossing London Bridge and entering the borough of Southwark, described in *Bradshaw's Illustrated Handbook to London and Its Environs as: 'one of the most animated parts of the metropolis, from the extent of the business carried on in this extensive locality'.* Lucy's research has also elicited that this area was the site of the Globe theatre ~ where the plays of William Shakespeare were acted. Had she walked these streets in the sixteenth century, as opposed to today, she might even have encountered the great man himself on the way to the theatre, clutching the quill-written pages of his latest piece. It is a thrilling thought.

Reaching the high street, Lucy pauses outside the Talbot Inn, to remind herself that this historic building was the *actual* location of the Tabard Inn, the staging post where Geoffrey Chaucer, Knight, and his twenty-nine pilgrims lodged on their way to Canterbury. And in a way, she reminds herself, she is also on a pilgrimage, to seek out the shrine of truth. It is always a pleasure to ally oneself with the great literary figures of the past.

As she advances towards her destination, her small nose is assailed by the smells of vinegar, leather, sulphur, brewing, glue, and from one small street she passes, the unexpected odour of strawberry jam.

Everything is unfamiliar, distinct, and different. Truly, she is in foreign territory!

On the corner of Dover Street and Blackman Street, a two-horse-drawn omnibus to Clapham and Lord Wellington clops past. A couple of men in bowler hats look down at her admiringly. Lucy tosses her head and ignores them. She is a modern girl, not for her the sly male glance, the calculating stare. She continues walking towards the white-towered church at the end of the street, checking the building numbers until she reaches Number 150 ~ which proves to be a butcher's shop, with joints of meat set out and hung in the window.

Lucy enters, picking her way daintily across the sawdust floor. She approaches the counter, where the butcher, who resembles every butcher she has ever encountered, being big, red-faced, with a bristly moustache and beefy sausage-fingers, is sharpening a vicious-looking knife on a grindstone.

"Well, good day, young lady," he says, carefully placing the knife down on a thick wooden chopping board and turning to face her. "Ain't you a sight for sore eyes. Nah then, wot can I get you? Nice bit of steak for your man's tea? Fry up a treat wiv an onion and a few p'tatoes. What d'you fink? I can do you a special price, coz I likes the look of yer pretty face."

Lucy dimples her refusal. "I'm sure that would be lovely, but I am here to find somebody," she says. "His name is Mr Francis Brooke. This is the last address I have for him. Do you recognise that name by any chance?"

The butcher folds his meaty arms and stares down at her. "I fink you'd better arsk Miss Leonora ~ she has the Dancing Academy upstairs. You can go straight up; there ain't no pupils. I know coz I'd hear them overhead if there was. Like a herd of bloomin' elephants they are."

Lucy recalls there was an advertisement for The Select Leonora Dance School on the wall outside the shop. She climbs the bare wooden steps and knocks at a door labelled *'Dance Academy: Lessons for Beginners and Experienced Dancers. 1/- an hour. Children to Adults. Special Rates for Couples. Enquire Within.'*

Lucy's knock is answered by a very short woman with very tall golden hair piled above her head in a series of random ringlets, cascades and curls, decorated with bright pink and green feathers. The effect is startling, especially when combined with a low-cut emerald-green silk dress, shiny red lips, pink cheeks and an armful of jangly silver bangles. She wears pink dancing pumps on her feet and carries a silver-topped stick, which she clasps in her be-ringed fingers as she peers up at Lucy.

"Good afternoon, young lady. You wish to inquire about dancing lessons, I presume?"

Lucy shakes her head. "No. Thank you. I'm looking for information about a certain individual, and hoping you can help me. His name is Mr Francis Brooke. Have you come across him by any chance?"

She shows the woman the photograph of the couple posing at the lych-gate. The intricately head-dressed woman's face immediately changes. Her colour fades, leaving two vivid spots of rouge on each cheek, and her eyes harden into icy points. She breathes in sharply, her grip on the stick tightening.

"And who are you?" she asks, her tone harsh, as she stares at the photograph in Lucy's hand.

"I am the person inquiring about him," Lucy says, smiling her most winning smile.

"Why are you inquiring, may I ask?"

"It is a private matter."

"I see. A private matter. Yes. Well, I can tell you that is certainly Francis Brooke. I'd know him anywhere. But I don't recognise the woman with him, though."

"She was his wife. She died a short while ago."

The woman laughs unpleasantly. "Was she now. His wife, you say? Ah. His wife. That is interesting. Because, you see, young woman, I am Mrs Leonora Brooke, his wife. I have been his wife for nine years. And as you can see, I'm still very much alive."

Lucy's jaw drops open. Her eyes widen in shock. "You ... you ... are his *wife*?" she stutters.

"Yes, you weren't expecting that, were you? I can see by the look on your face. But it is true. I can show you my marriage certificate if you don't believe me. But as for where he is now, I can't help you there, because I haven't seen nor heard from Mr Francis Brooke for a long time. In fact, I haven't seen hide nor hair of the scoundrel since he ran off with all our savings and the profits from the Dance Academy!"

Lucy continues to gape at her, words failing.

"Well, make up your mind, young woman," says the first Mrs Brooke sharply, tapping her stick impatiently on the floor. "I'm not going to stand here all day. If you want to hear about my marriage to that man, either come in, or else be on your way."

Lucy hesitates no longer. She goes into the flat.

Daylight is beginning to slide from the sky as Lucy Landseer leaves the dance studio. She picks up an omnibus outside the Elephant and Castle Tavern, surrendering herself to the swaying rhythm, while letting her thoughts wander where they take her. What she'd thought was a simple case of reassuring an anxious and grieving client has turned into something much darker and far more complex.

Reaching her consulting room at last, she writes a hasty note to Rosalind Whitely, requesting her to call round at her earliest convenience. She stresses the importance of keeping the prospective meeting from her stepfather but decides not to reveal why she is making the request.

In the meantime, Lucy decides to inquire about the legal position of a man who marries two women, whilst still married to a third. It is like the plot of a sensational novel. Or the sort of scandalous, immoral play that would generate strictures from certain high-minded theatre critics and be closed down by order of the Lord Chancellor.

Never had Lucy imagined, when beginning upon her professional career as a consulting private detective, that she would find herself investigating such a complex case in real life. Her fictitious heroine Belle Batchelor (and her faithful sidekick Harris) have never had to tackle anything as extraordinary. Lucy is beginning to realise that, while in fiction one controls what happens, in real life the plot twists and turns in ways that are beyond even her vivid imagination.

And yet. Gradually, step by step, the narrative is working towards the final outcome. Will there be more revelations upon the way? Who can tell? Her next move, she decides, is to turn her attention to the central character in the investigation. *Yes indeed, Mr Francis Brooke*, Lucy thinks, *you may hide your past from the world, and from your wives, past and present, but not from me. I am going to expose you for who you really are.*

****

London at night. A place of infinite and bewitching variety, where friends, strangers and thousands of visitors are also part of the entertainment. Enchantment pours from every brightly-lit public house, restaurant and theatrical venue. Step inside this palace of varieties and view the gay scene for yourself. Here is a gas-lit fairyland, peopled by merry revellers in various stages of intoxication.

Chandeliers sparkle brightly, picking out the gold paint adorning boxes and balconies. Supper tables spill across the auditorium floor. This evening the Varieties Music Hall is full ~ one thousand, two hundred patrons are eating, drinking, promenading or just leaning on various ledges watching the acts and each other.

The newly built proscenium arch separates audience from performers, giving the headliners and other acts a sense of distance, and hopefully adding to their safety. Music hall audiences know what they enjoy, and what to do if they don't. It is not so long ago that Florrie Firkins, a woman whose prime was long behind her, was hauled off the stage, in full warble, by a disgruntled audience and unceremoniously tossed out of the front door into the street.

Tonight, however, the Variety plays host to some of the best of contemporary entertainment. Here is Micky Mokey standing in the wings, enjoying a cigarette before it is his turn to go on stage. He watches Little Azella performing her routine. Even though he has seen it countless times, he still has his heart in his mouth.

A spotlight directs the audience's attention up to the ceiling, where a tiny female figure in tights and a sparkling waistcoat is seated on a high catwalk. There is a roll of drums and to gasps from the audience below, the figure leaps. But instead of plunging to her death, the tiny acrobat soars to even new heights, balanced precariously on a practically invisible wire.

Little Azella is a creature of air. She pirouettes, spins, walks up invisible stairs. It is all an illusion of course ~ shadowy figures on the floor act as counterweights, working in concert to keep the ropes taught so that she can turn somersaults or fly straight up into a grand jeté.

Her act ends with a final dramatic leap straight out over the heads of the audience, causing the diners at the front to duck down as she passes above them. Light as a feather, she balances on the rim of one of the boxes, then turns and bows, holding out her arms in a final farewell before being lifted down into the darkness to roars of applause.

Micky Mokey feels his shoulders untense. Every night he is afraid that an accident could happen; that Little Azella might fall down into the pit, thrown to her death by some careless stagehand not paying attention, and end up a tiny, crumpled heap of sequins and tinsel on the wooden floor.

He has just got his breath back when he hears his music being played. Squaring his shoulders, he sets his top hat to a jaunty angle, sticks his gloved hands into his pearl-grey frock coat pockets, and saunters nonchalantly out onto the stage to loud clapping (and a few boos) from the audience.

The small orchestra strikes up with 'I'm a Pall Mall Johnnie with a Roving Eye' as Micky Mokey launches into the popular song, encouraging the audience to join in the chorus:

"I've got no home,
I just have to roam,
So, give me champagne or I'll die, tiddly aye tye."

It is pretty mawkish stuff, but they love it, and he has to sing the number twice more before he is allowed to leave the stage. After a second appearance by both artistes, Micky Mokey and his lodging-house companion venture out into the balmy evening for some supper, before their next show.

The fragrant smell of frying fish lures them to one stall, where they pay for a paper of succulent fish pieces, going on to buy two baked potatoes from another stall.

They take their food to a quiet doorway to enjoy in peace.

"You still got some of that reward money left, then?" Little Azella asks through a mouthful of potato. "You done well there, Micky."

Micky Mokey sucks his greasy fingers. "Still don't know what he's doing in town, though," he says. "But I mean to find out."

Little Azella shakes her head, causing a small rain of glitter to fall on the step. "Why d'you want to do that, Micky? Leave well alone is my motter. Let the past lie. You did a good deed; you got a reward. The man didn't reckernise you, as you said. Walk away. No good can come of raking over cold ashes."

Micky Mokey doesn't respond. Mainly because he is very fond of Little Azella, and he wouldn't want to go offside with her. If you share a poky lodging-house room with someone week in week out, you soon learn many things about them and about their backstory. Mind you, everybody in the entertainment business has a backstory. Mostly bad, which is why they are either running away from it, or mentally re-living it over again, but in a different time and place.

Little Azella's story is that she is a Jewess, who had to leave her community when, at six years old, on the back of being taken to a circus, she decided to become a female acrobat, a decision that caused so much consternation that her parents were advised by their rabbi either to lock her up or put her out onto the street.

In the end, after years of wrangling, she made the decision for them, making her way to London, where the fabled gold-paved streets proved to be a bit of a disappointment, but where she was eventually discovered by Luigi, the Great Stupendo, who taught her the ways of the rope and trapeze when he discovered her, destitute and living in a non-golden alley. Even though she is now topping the bill every night, the heartbreak has never healed. Someday, she says, she will go back to Leicester, a fine lady in a carriage and show them all!

Micky Mokey always smiles whenever she says this, and replies, 'Yes, of course you will,' but inside, he knows it won't happen. One day, Little Azella will be performing her act as usual, when she'll step out into thin air. Only this time, there won't be any rope to save her, and she will fall to earth, like a sweet bird that has been shot, and that will be the end of her dreams, which is, in a way, a metaphor for all of them.

But until that day, Micky Mokey has plans. He is determined to find out what Sherborne Harbinger is doing in the city. He knows where the man is staying, so tomorrow he is going to position himself outside the hotel and follow him when he appears. From his first sight of the man in the audience, the memory of him has been an itch on Micky Mokey's brain. It is like a door you thought you'd locked suddenly opening on a cold night. He cannot ignore it, whatever the consequences. Walking away is not an option. Not yet, anyway.

And sure enough, next morning, here he is, dressed in a sombre dark suit, with a top hat set low down on his brow. The outfit has been borrowed from the music hall's costume department and is a little too big for him, but he still looks the perfect replica of a smart city gent. He has strategically applied some stage makeup, to darken his eyebrows and give him the appearance of an incipient moustache.

Mickey Mokey greets the liveried doorman and, assuming an air of confident authority, enters the Excelsior Hotel, which at this time of day, smells of coffee and fried bacon. He approaches the front desk, where he inquires after Mr Sherborne Harbinger, a guest, in a business-like tone of voice.

"I am sorry sir, the gentleman in question has just left," the desk clerk says. "I am surprised you did not run into him."

Uttering his thanks, Micky Mokey turns and heads quickly for the door, setting off in the opposite direction. People are pushing their way like badly organised armies, but after a few hectic minutes, he spies his quarry up ahead. He is on his own; the miserable young girl is not with him this time. Micky Mokey edges closer, always keeping two people apart. He sees Sherborne Harbinger enter a coffee house and follows him inside.

Harbinger goes straight across the room to a table at the back, where he is greeted by another man with a sour face and an unwelcoming expression. At the sight of him, Micky Mokey sucks in his breath. He selects the next table, sliding himself into a seat, with his back to the two men. He orders coffee and a round of toast. Then he helps himself to one of the daily newspapers, and using it as a screen, leans in to the adjacent conversation.

"So, little brother, I hear you have been visiting Aunt Euphemia behind my back," Arthur Harbinger says.

"I was unaware that I had to seek your permission to visit my own relation," Sherborne Harbinger retorts tartly.

"It will do you no good to sneak round there and ingratiate yourself," Arthur Harbinger says. "She doesn't like you. Or your children. All you are doing, little brother, is making her even more determined to cut you out of her Will."

"And you know this for a fact, do you? You have had sight of her Will? How have you managed to do that?" Sherborne snaps.

A waitress brings coffee to their table. Arthur Harbinger stirs sugar into his cup. "Oh, I have my sources, little brother. Aunt is not going to fall for your tricks, I can assure you."

"Oh really? Is she not? Well, I have to inform you, she made a great pet of Harriet t'other day and indeed she has begged me ~ begged me, to let her visit again. Which I intend to do. What a shame you have no dear children to lisp and prattle at your knee and endear themselves to a rich dying aunt. But then, you were never one for the ladies, were you, Arthur. Or children in general. I remember how you used to torment our little sister when we were young."

"As did you, I recall. Far more than ever I did, since I was away at boarding school for most of the time. I warn you, Sherborne," Arthur Harbinger hisses, jabbing across the table at his brother with his spoon to emphasise the words. "We agreed that all visits to the Chelsea house would be made jointly. You have broken our agreement. You will not steal a march on me. Not now, not ever. I am the elder. I inherit first."

"Pooh, stuff and nonsense," Sherborne Harbinger scoffs. He gulps down his coffee and rises to his feet. "If this is all you wanted to see me about, Arthur, then I'm off. My family is waiting. We are going to visit the British Museum, and then after luncheon, I think I shall take the children round to visit their dear great aunt at the Chelsea house that one day will be mine. They can impress her with their knowledge of the Assyrians. I'm sure she will be delighted to see them again. Good day to you, sir."

Micky Mokey waits a few seconds, then pays for his toast and leaves. Crossing the road, he saunters off towards Oxford Street, hands in pockets, the picture of a perfect city swell. After what he has just overheard, he has a lot to think about. He is also slightly dreading arriving at the music hall. Ever since the night he serenaded her, Liza-Lou keeps seeking him out and simpering foolishly at him, much to the displeasure of the assistant stage-manager. Micky Mokey has told Liza-Lou in no uncertain terms that he is not interested in her, but she refuses to believe him. It is causing difficulties with her putative swain, who has miscued him a couple of times. Possibly accidentally, but probably not.

As he skilfully weaves his way around the shopping crowds and other pavement detritus, he thinks back to the little scene he has just witnessed in the coffee house. Once again, he was not recognised at all. Astonishing! At this point, Mikey Mokey's good angel, who sometimes goes by the name of Little Azella, tells him to leave it there and not push his luck. However, there is a certain thrill in placing himself in a risky situation ~ he guesses it is very much the same thrill that Little Azella feels when she launches herself off the wire into thin air. So no, he isn't going to listen.

****

Miss Lucy Landseer, on the other hand, has been doing a great deal of listening. Not to mention thinking and making notes. And as a result, she is quite prepared when her young client Rosalind Whitely knocks on the door of the consulting room. Lucy greets her, and ushers her to the clientele chair (now furnished with a rather attractive Chinese print cushion) before bringing her own chair (un-cushioned) round so that she can sit next to her.

The client lifts her veil, revealing a face even more worn than last time they met, her eyes red-rimmed and haunted. Lucy's heart goes out to her. To be so young, and so unhappy. And she is about to add even more unhappiness to the burden already carried.

"Before I hear what you have to tell me, Miss Landseer, I must tell you of a development in my own life. My stepfather has informed me that it is his intention to sell the house. It is his house now, you know. He inherited it from my mother. He has decided it is far too big for two people, too expensive to run, and the number of servants is surplus to our requirements.

"He has already got rid of two of the maids, who have been with the family for years. I am trying to be reasonable, to accord with his wishes, but it is the home I have lived in from a child. All my memories are there. I am finding it very hard ~ very hard indeed, Miss Landseer," her voice falters. She takes a handkerchief from her bag and mops her eyes.

Lucy waits patiently, and in silence, for her client to recover her equilibrium.

"I believe that I told you I have been left a small inheritance from my parents, which I have offered as a contribution to the running of the house, but my stepfather says it is not nearly enough. Today, even as we speak, he is visiting an estate agent to discover how much the house would sell for. He mentions moving out of London altogether ~ Cheltenham, Gloucester, perhaps, or another town in that area. He says he can easily find work in such a place. He speaks about renting a room in London temporarily while he changes location and employment. He does not mention me in any of his plans. Oh, Miss Landseer, the thought of leaving London, of being unable to visit my dear parents' graves, never to place flowers upon them ~ the pain is so great. What is to become of me?"

Lucy leans forward and places her hand upon the trembling arm of the young woman sitting opposite. "I promise you, Miss Whitely, that you will NOT have to leave your family home, unless or until it is of your own volition," she says firmly. "Now, dry your eyes. I shall tell you why I am so confident in my pronouncement. But I warn you, you must be brave, and prepare yourself, for I am the bearer of shocking news: The sale of the house cannot go ahead because your stepfather does *not* own it. Mr Brooke has a wife still living ~ and I have met her and spoken to her."

Rosalind Whitely's young face drains of all colour. She starts swaying in her seat, her eyes rolling upwards, wide and unfocussed. Lucy leaps from her chair, and just manages to catch her as she slumps forward. She lies her client gently on the floor, then goes to fill the kettle. Tea, strong and hot, with plenty of sugar is the best medicine for shock. And then, after tea, the construction of a plan.

****

Meanwhile, Detective Sergeant Jack Cully is taking his young protégé, Constable Tom Williams, for an instructive stroll. He is aware that the young man played an important part at the outset of the investigation into Robertson's stolen body. He wrote an exemplary report. He accompanied Cully on a site visit and to various other places.

Now that the search for a perpetrator seems to have petered out and the investigation has been closed, Cully does not want the young officer to get discouraged. The detective division is in need of new blood. Several officers have indicated they are intending to retire at the end of the year. Detective Inspector Stride is always going to retire at the end of every year, although so far, he has never done so.

As they walk side by side down the street, at the pace known to every police officer in the country as 'proceeding', Cully shares some of his professional insights, picked up during his long career in the Metropolitan Police Force.

"Whenever you are called to a crime scene, it is vitally important that you go through the proper procedures. They never vary. First, always note the position of the body. Make a sketch of it ~ if you can. Make a note of exactly where you found the body, the clothes the deceased is wearing and the surface they are lying on. Then, note all the objects and items close to the body.

"At some time in the future, you may be called upon to give evidence at a coroner's inquest. If you have made careful and thorough notes, you will be well placed to do so. I have attended many inquests where the officer who found the body did not make notes and has subsequently forgotten all the small details that might cause the coroner to decide the death was criminal in nature. If it is deemed accidental, because no good evidence has been submitted to indicate the contrary, we cannot proceed to investigate and so justice is not done."

They proceed across Trafalgar Square, the tourist crowds parting before them, like a shoal of minnows sensing the presence of predators. Nobody wants to get in the way of police officers pursuing their duty. After all, you might get caught up in something unsavoury that wasn't your fault.

Cully continues, "I'd also advise you to keep your report as simple as possible. And as clear. I've observed you have a good written style. That will help you when presenting your evidence publicly in the witness-box."

Cully decides not to share some of Robertson's more esoteric offerings. He recalls the time the police surgeon referred to an 'apoplectic extravasation' rather than a blood clot. Another time, it was a 'contusion' not a bruise. The Middlesex coroner was neither impressed nor amused.

Constable Williams nods. "I understand." He hesitates, seems as if he is about to say more, but then closes his mouth firmly.

Cully notes the gesture. "Go on, Tom, what do you want to say?"

The constable takes a deep breath. "I have been thinking about the man I found and how we've stopped looking for the person who murdered him. I've been thinking about it a lot, Mr Cully, and it disturbs me."

Cully has a notion where this conversation is going. It is almost as if he is listening to his younger self, railing at the inability of his superiors to track down a man who'd brutally strangled a child prostitute and left her in a sordid alleyway, where young Constable Cully had discovered her. He was only a beat constable at that time, just starting out, and their incompetence and reluctance to bring to justice the man who'd taken her life, because, at the end of the day, it was only a twelve-year old girl, was one of the driving forces that had convinced him to apply to join the detective division.

They reach Pall Mall East and proceed towards Haymarket. It is easier to talk while walking. Side by side rather than face to face. Cully stares straight ahead, waiting for the script that he could've written to be spoken.

"You see, Mr Cully, it strikes me that there's more than one way to look at what they call justice. If you're the man who doesn't get caught, then justice means getting away with your crime. If you never have to pay for what you did, why should you care about what's right ~ as far as you're concerned, whatever you get away with is right. That is what justice means to you. Do you understand me?"

"Yes, I do."

"And for the man you murdered, the life you cut short, that sort of justice means nothing. Nothing to his family and friends. They need to see the man who committed the crime in front of a judge and jury. They need to hear sentence delivered and punishment handed out. If there is to be no punishment, no trial, then where is their justice? Maybe I'm being muddled, I don't know."

"You are being very clear, Tom. Very clear indeed."

"The man I found that night, someone ended his life. He was about my age. He had everything to live for. Why should they not face a trial? Is that not an injustice?"

Cully stops walking, turns, and looks into the honest and indignant face. "Yes, I agree, Tom," he says quietly. "But sometimes, it just doesn't happen like that. If you want to join the detective division, you need to take it on board, or it will drive you to despair. We do not always 'win', because we are dealing with human nature, and human nature goes sideways, and crookedly, and not in a straight line.

"People get away with crimes. Big ones, small petty ones. We can only investigate and explore and deduce as best we can. This is a huge city, and there are many places a criminal can hide and a lot of ways of covering up their crime. I know you are disappointed. So am I. Whenever a young man or woman loses their lives in a violent way, I grieve for the future they will no longer have. But I am convinced that somewhere along the line, the people who take those lives will be punished. We may never know who they are, but I believe it will happen. Maybe not in this world, but it will happen."

The constable sucks in his bottom lip. "I wish I could believe that too, Mr Cully."

"I think you will come round to believing it in time, constable. The main thing is to make sure that at every stage, we do the very best we can to catch the wrongdoers. And if one slips through the net, then so be it. Someone will catch him further along the line."

Cully places a kindly hand on Constable Williams' shoulder. "And now, we have come far enough. I think a drink and a bite to eat is called for. I see a coffee-stall up ahead. How about a cup of coffee before we go back? I don't know about you, but I am parched from all this walking."

Upon their return, they discover the pale spindly young parliamentary clerk who identified the body once again seated in the outer office. He rises at their entrance and stands awkwardly, hands dangling by his sides, waiting to be acknowledged. Cully greets him in a kindly manner and inquires after his health. The Replacement shrugs. He has walked here without stopping for lunch. He seems to be missing more and more meals at the moment. And thinking more and more. The need to discover who killed his friend has taken him over, body and soul.

Every day he trudges from his lodgings to his place of work without really being aware of his journey, repeating the same process in reverse at the end of the day. He dresses in the morning, undresses in the evening. Work is done in between the times. Sometimes, he lies awake, watching moonlight chasing shadows across the ceiling.

His mind is always elsewhere. Time folds back on itself, as if a fault line has opened up. The present falls away. He wanders through the ruins of the past, when his friend was alive. They meet and discuss matters. He remembers his eyes, the slant of his cheekbones. He has never felt so close to his dead friend; he has never felt so alone. In the dark of his head, he realises that his friend will always stay with him, even though he will never see him again.

"I recall you said that I might speak with the officer who found my friend's body," he says hesitantly. "When might I speak with him?"

Cully indicates Constable Williams. "You are in luck. This is the very officer. You may speak with him right now. Tom ~ take our friend to the interview room."

The Replacement turns to face the sturdy young constable, who regards him with wary sympathy. "If you'd like to follow me, sir," he says, leading the way.

The afternoon sunlight streams in through the grimy window, lighting the whitewashed walls and the simple wooden table and chairs. They sit down either side of the table. An awkward silence falls.

"How can I help you? What do you want to know?"

The Replacement frowns, works his mouth. "Can you paint a picture for me. Exactly as you saw him on that night. Everything you remember. Leave no detail out."

The young constable begins to speak. As his voice rises and falls, the Replacement closes his eyes, letting the words wash over him. He tries to see the picture being described, but it is as if a curtain has fallen between them. Eventually, when the constable stops speaking, he opens his eyes and raises his head.

"I went to the place a few days ago to see it for myself. I met a man there, a short man with a pock-marked face. He could be the foreman: he carried a set of keys. Or the developer. Maybe he knows something about my friend's murder? Perhaps he was there on the night and saw something that might help catch his killer? Will you question him?"

The constable shifts awkwardly on the hard wooden chair. "I wish we could. But you see, we can't. Not now. The investigation has been closed. Orders from Detective Inspector Stride. There is no evidence. Nobody saw the attack. Nobody has come forward with any information, other than you. So even if this man does know something, it is unlikely Scotland Yard would re-open the case.

"Also, your friend's parents have said they see no point in the investigation going forward. His mother has been badly affected, and his father does not wish for any more suffering to be inflicted on her and the family. They have applied to remove the body for burial in their own town."

The Replacement stares at him. "But a man has been murdered, in cold blood. Someone must be held accountable. There has to be justice for his life surely?"

Constable Williams pulls a face, "My thoughts exactly. And I said as much to the detective sergeant not half an hour ago."

"And what did he say?"

"He said: sometimes, you never know who committed a crime. You never see justice done. But he also said he is sure people do get punished, even though we may never know it. I am very sorry. That is all I can tell you."

"It is not enough," the Replacement mutters, his jaw tightening. He feels a pain in the place where tears come. A heaviness in his heart.

The two young men sit on, both trying to find words that elude them. In the distance, a church bell chimes. A cab goes by. There are jagged shouts from somewhere deep in the building. A background noise of people. The Replacement rubs his forehead with the back of his hand. His mouth tastes of ashes. He had thought by speaking about the death, by hearing about it, he might understand, and could leave his dark thoughts behind. Instead, he is left with a feeling of bitterness, a sense of even more loss than he felt before.

Eventually, when it is clear that there is nothing more to be said on either side, the Replacement rises. He steps out into the hot noisy street, blinking dazedly in the sunshine. People rush past him, bright and busy. The world continues on its uncaring way, frighteningly impossible in its thinness. He feels cheated. He twists through the crowd, sensing that he is changing. He is not sure what he is becoming.

****

It is hard enough facing one's own demise. It is even harder when it is framed by regular visitations from eager-eyed relatives, under whose superficial solicitude lies a cold calculation of one's proximity to the reaper's scythe. So thinks Euphemia Harbinger, as she lies in her bed, her blue-veined hands encased in woollen mittens, for even in the heat of the late afternoon, she still feels a chill. She is so worn out by the competitive caring of her greedy nephews; even her initial interest in the two children has faded. She would like to spend more time with the girl Harriet, who piques her interest, but it has been made clear that the children come as a pair.

This afternoon, she has endured the boy's recital of the kings and queens of England, applauded by his doting father, followed by a list of the things they saw in the British Museum. Her days of interest in the Assyrians being long past, if it ever existed in the first place, Euphemia Harbinger had listened with polite indifference. Out of the corner of her eye, she'd observed the girl, who sat mute on the sofa, crumbling a shortbread biscuit and staring at her feet. Occasionally, she tried to interject some observation or other, but was quickly shut down by the two male members of her family.

It was a short, uncomfortable visit, and then, ten minutes after the family departed, the older brother had arrived, unaccompanied, but laden with chocolates she could no longer stomach, and a bunch of white lilies, whose smell always reminded her of funerals. She wonders idly whether it is a subtle message? The old woman sighs. It is difficult work, this dying. She glances at the little bedside clock. Now it is 6.30, almost time for the mush that constitutes her dinner to appear. And even as her brain takes this in, her ears hear the unexpected clang of the letterbox downstairs in the hall, and a few minutes later, the maid steps into the room carrying a letter.

"This letter has just been delivered, ma'am. It is marked urgent, so I decided to bring it up right away."

Euphemia Harbinger levers herself upright with an effort. Then, taking the teaspoon from her saucer, she works a corner of the envelope open and extracts a sheet of closely written notepaper. As she reads the contents of her letter, her eyes narrow and her mouth sets in a determined line. So that is the lie of the land, is it? Reaching the end, she picks up the little bell that summons the housekeeper, and requests writing material to be brought to her chamber.

"Come back in ten minutes," she orders. "I will need you to post three letters for me. It is imperative that they go tonight. And I'll take a little glass of sherry wine with my meal. No point in leaving the bottle to gather dust in the pantry."

****

It is the morrow, and breakfast is being served at the Excelsior Hotel. Eggs march in serried silver-cupped ranks across the mahogany buffet. Domed dishes protect kedgeree, bacon, kidneys and sausages. Toast stands racked to attention. Butter and assorted preserves lie dormant in small glass dishes. It is like a military manoeuvre, supervised by the hotel under-manager with ferocious side-whiskers and a black tailcoat.

The guests help themselves. There is an air of relaxation and enjoyment, for most of the guests are tourists. Copies of Bradshaw are being scrutinised, and discussions held as to where to go on this lovely sunny day, with the smell of freshly brewed coffee backgrounding the various conversations.

Only at one table is none of the above taking place. Here, breakfast is being gulped down at speed and in complete silence. The reason for this undue haste can be explained by a letter in the pocket of the *paterfamilias*, received this morning by the 7.30 post, summoning him to his aunt's house.

Scarcely has the last mouthful been swallowed, when Sherborne Harbinger rises, gestures to his children to go and get ready, and orders his wife to remain in her room with the baby, to await developments.

"This is it, Charlotte," he says. "She is going at last! And Arthur has been cut out of the Will ~ that much is abundantly clear!" and with a barely concealed smile of triumph, he hurries to get his hat, coat and gloves.

The three Harbingers barrel along the early-morning street, fighting the shop workers and street-sellers, tripping over baskets of flowers, being cursed by small child shoe-blacks, until finally they reach the environs of Chelsea. Suddenly, Harbinger stops, his body stiffening. The instinctive reaction of a man sighting a natural enemy, for there, just going in through the gate of his aunt's house, is his brother Arthur.

Sherborne grabs his offspring by various elbows and propels them at speed towards the house. They arrive just as Arthur Harbinger is being ushered over the threshold by the maid. Sherborne almost flings the twins into the hallway, hissing: "What the hell do you think you are doing here?"

Arthur Harbinger calmly divests himself of his coat and hat, then turns to face his irate, red-faced sibling. "I was invited by our beloved aunt to attend her this morning. And you, little brother ~ what brings you hot-foot from your cheap hotel?"

Sherborne produces a letter and waves it in his brother's face. "I have a letter inviting me."

"As do I," Arthur Harbinger says calmly. "So, we have both been invited then. I presume it is about the event that we have been awaiting. Let us therefore attend our aunt and witness her last moments upon earth with suitable solemnity. I suggest your children remain in the hallway."

In reply, Sherborne pushes the twins past Arthur, saying to the astonished maid: "Show us into our aunt's presence, at once."

The warring tribe follow the servant into the sitting room. Sunlight streams through the window. A soft August breeze flutters the net curtain. In its cage, the grey parrot bobs and bows. Aunt Euphemia, wrapped in a soft blue cashmere shawl, reclines on the sofa, watching its antics. She glances up sharply as the visitors enter.

"Why, dearest aunt," Arthur gushes, "You are out of bed? Really? And looking … so well?"

Sherborne applies a hand to Hanover's back, propelling him towards the sofa. Hanover, well-schooled in the art of inheritance-seeking, and a chip off the old paternal block, makes a low bow accompanied by an unctuous smile. Harriet goes straight over to the cage to talk to the parrot, who turns delighted somersaults at the sight of her.

"Be quiet Charlotte, you stupid woman," it shouts. (Sherborne attempts to drown it out with a fit of fake coughing.)

"I have summoned you both here," Euphemia Harbinger says, when some semblance of order has eventually been restored, "because I have recently received a letter. From your sister, Wilhelmina."

Absolute, stunned silence. Arthur looks at Sherborne, who looks back. Both are nonplussed.

"Yes, indeed," the old woman continues, her face wiped of all expression. "She has written a long and very nice letter, inquiring after my health and apologising for not coming to see me sooner, but, as she says, neither of her brothers bothered to inform her that I was in failing health."

She stares at Arthur. "I thought you told me you were going to write to your sister?"

"Oh. I. Well. Business affairs ..." he stammers.

Sherborne frowns. "But you said, dearest aunt, that you had yourself written to Wilhelmina, but received no reply to your letter."

"But now I have," the old lady snaps. "She has been travelling with a companion, and the letter has only just been forwarded to her. No thanks to either of you, eh?"

Arthur's eyes narrow. "Wait a bit. Wait a bit. Not so fast. How do we know that it IS her? Anybody could have signed their name 'Wilhelmina'. Perhaps the letter is a fake, from someone who wishes you harm. Maybe they just want to get their hands on your money. Such things are all too commonplace in this wicked world. The person signing themselves Wilhelmina might, in reality, be the leader of a gang of swindlers. I believe you should not regard it as genuine."

In reply, the old lady hands him the sheet of writing paper. "See for yourself. I presume you recognise your own sister's handwriting?"

Arthur Harbinger reads the letter, bites his underlip, then passes the letter to his younger brother. Both men's faces exhibit all the terror of free fall, as if a comfortable and predictable world had suddenly become an abyss.

"She says she is staying in London at the moment, and wishes to visit you," Arthur says in a strangled tone.

"Indeed, she does, and I have replied expressing my desire to see her too."

"When does this visit take place? I think, as head of the family, I should also attend."

The old woman gives him a shrewd glance. "In view of the lie you told to me, I do not invite either of you to be present. I wish to speak to your sister alone. And now, I think it is time for my nap. Rose will show you out. Good morning."

The old lady sits back, sighs and closes her eyes tightly. The brothers rise. Sherborne hisses at the children to stop whatever they are doing and accompany him. Hanover, like a well-trained lapdog, follows his father out of the room, but Harriet waits by the window, her gaze fixed on the old lady's face. Slowly, one eye opens, swivels round the room, spots her standing there, and closes again.

Harriet retrieves her bonnet and is shown out into the street, where she finds her father and her uncle having a furious argument on the pavement. Hanover is busy teasing a small black and white cat that has appeared out of somewhere.

"I blame you, Arthur!" Sherborne exclaims. "You are the eldest. It was your duty to give Wilhelmina her share of the estate. If you had obeyed his last suggestion, this situation would never have arisen."

"Oh, you think so?" Arthur sneers. "As I recall, little brother, it was your idea to cut all ties with her. For richer, for even richer, I think was what you said. Blood may be thicker than water, but gold is even thicker still, I believe you also said. And now, thanks to you, our sister is about to step in and cut us both out. You think aunt will leave us a farthing, after Wilhelmina has poured her poison into her ear? So much for all your big plans for your boy's future!"

Hanover catches these last words and starts to wail. Sherborne gnashes his teeth. "What to do? What to do?" he exclaims, striding backwards and forwards. "Should we wait outside and catch her before she goes in?"

"We could, but sadly, we don't know when that will be, do we? And even if we found out, what should we say to her? '*Hello little sister, how unexpectedly nice to meet you after all this time. Sorry about your share of the inheritance; we spent it, but please don't hold it against us, and can you tell aunt you don't want any of her money, thank you.*' You think she will just forgive and forget? Did she ever forgive and forget? You think she won't go straight to our aunt and tell her what we did? No, we have to come up with a plan."

Sherborne gathers himself together. "You are right. A plan. That is what we must do. I shall go back to my hotel and work on it. I'll write to you when I have concocted something."

"Do that, little brother and make sure it is watertight. Because we are on the cusp of inheriting a great deal of money and jewels, let alone a fine house. And I for one, am not going to allow it to slip through my fingers."

They part company. Sherborne chivvies his reluctant offspring back to the hotel, where they are immediately told to go to their rooms. From her room, Harriet hears her father shouting at her mother, and the accompanying sobbing of the baby. Eventually, when the noise has died down, she gets out her notebook, turns to the back, and begins writing.

The bond between parent and child is supposed to be one of the strongest upon earth, for it is forged upon the natural instincts of the one to love and protect the other, receiving love and obedience in return. But even the strongest of bonds can break, under extreme pressure, especially when stretched beyond the limit of their holding capacity.

Having written a brief note explaining why she has decided to quit her family forever, Harriet packs a few things and quietly opens her bedroom door. Her father ordered her to go to her room. She does not recall being told to stay there, though. She tiptoes down the stairs, strolls casually past the concierge desk, and goes out into the sunshine.

The day is pleasantly warm. Harriet sets her face away from the hotel and begins walking. It is wonderful to be out on her own, taking in the sounds and sights without a heavy hand on her shoulder propelling her at speed past interesting things. Every now and then she stops in her tracks and just looks all round her. This is the great city of London, she tells herself, where prophets walked the streets, where angels gathered on gable ends. If she listens hard, she can hear their wings beating in the still air, so many feathers on the breath of God.

Eventually, Harriet arrives at her destination. She selects a suitable doorway and sets up camp. As soon as it grows dark, she will make her move. There is a small sash window on the ground floor, whose catch has been slid to one side. It was done earlier this morning, while nobody was taking any notice of her. All she has to do now is quietly slide up the window and climb over the sill. It is a great big house; nobody will know she is there.

Harriet is about to become a ghost in someone else's life.

****

The lunchtime gong sounds in the hallway of the Excelsior Hotel, causing Charlotte Harbinger to scurry out of her room and knock at Harriet's door. When there is no reply, she opens the door and steps into the room, where the explanation for the lack of response becomes clear: there is no Harriet. She progresses to Hanover's room and repeats the procedure. Hanover is present, but once again, no Harriet. The assumption is made that she must have gone ahead to have her luncheon. Hanover, his mother, and the baby progress to the dining room, where Sherborne is helping himself to cut pork pie, ham, cheese, salads and bread, unaware that his family is currently minus one member.

"Is Harriet here?" Charlotte Harbinger asks, looking distractedly round the dining room. "I do not see her. She is not in her room either."

Sherborne takes his plate to the family table. "Why is she not in her room? I thought I told both children to remain in their rooms until I said otherwise."

"I stayed in my room, Papa," Hanover says virtuously, adding, "Perhaps she's run away to sea?"

His father stares disapprovingly at him. "Is that supposed to be amusing, Hanover? Because it is not. Girls don't run away to sea. Now Charlotte, give me a straight answer to a simple question ~ where is Harriet? You are in charge of the children, are you not?"

Charlotte Harbinger gapes at him. "I ... I ... do not know where she is."

Sherborne Harbinger rolls his eyes ceiling-wards and pulls out his chair. "Well, I am not going to let her absence spoil my luncheon. I suggest we all help ourselves from the buffet and get on with our meal. I am sure Harriet will appear at some point."

But she does not. At the end of lunch, Sherborne stands up and addresses his wife.

"Hanover and I are now going to visit Westminster Abbey."

"Should we not look for Harriet first, dear?" his wife suggests tentatively.

"Harriet is hiding in the hotel. It is not the first time she has secreted herself somewhere, is it? I expect she will reappear by this evening for her supper, when she will face the punishment she deserves. Come Hanover, you are not going to miss the chance to see some tombs of famous people, just because your sister is playing another of her silly games."

They leave. By the time they return, however, Charlotte Harbinger will have found Harriet's note and subsequently been informed by the desk manager that he is pretty sure he saw a young girl who resembled her daughter leave the hotel earlier in the day. Needless to say, her mother will be in a state of nervous collapse and have taken to her bed. A search of the immediate neighbourhood is organised by the hotel staff, but fails to come up with any Harriet, leaving Sherborne Harbinger with no alternative but to report his daughter to the local constabulary as a 'Missing Person', an act that he does with great reluctance.

****

While Sherborne and his son are trekking around Westminster Abbey, looking at the tombs of dead people, Euphemia Harbinger, who is not yet of their number, sits on the sofa in her sitting room, looking at the grey parrot. Rose, the housekeeper is feeding and cleaning the bird, and is being treated to a stream of 'interesting' remarks that once again throw a most unfortunate light upon the home life of her nephew Sherborne and his family.

The old lady takes a mordant delight in listening to the verbal indiscretions of the bird. Its cawing comments contrast with the unctuous civility of its owner. When one's end is approaching closer every day, pleasure has to be found where it can. Once, she received it via the seductive words of her suitors. Now, the gnomic utterances of the parrot have taken over.

"Get along with you, ugly child!" the parrot squawks, as Rose replaces its water bowl. *"I wish you'd never been born!"*

Rose closes the cage door and the bird sidles across to its food. *"Harriet, go to bed at once! You will have no supper tonight!"* it says, spearing a grape.

The doorbell rings. The old woman's mouth tightens. Rose gives her a questioning glance.

"I can say you are not receiving, madam?"

Euphemia Harbinger rearranges her hands in her lap. "No, let them come. Perhaps it will be the little girl again. I enjoyed seeing her ~ she reminds me of myself."

Rose goes to answer the bell.

She reappears seconds later to announce Arthur Harbinger.

The old woman sighs. "You again?"

"Good day, dearest aunt," Arthur says, forcing an affable expression onto his dour features, where it fights for control with his normal one. "I trust I find you still in the best of health, as you were this morning?"

"Hardly. I am one day nearer my end. Now, sit down Arthur, you are making the room untidy standing there. I suppose you have come back to try to get me to tell you when your sister is visiting, so that you can stick your nose in, am I right?"

Arthur Harbinger reels back in his chair, as if struck by a mighty blow. "Nothing, NOTHING is further from the truth, dear aunt. I am DELIGHTED that Wilhelmina has chosen, after all this time, to fulfil at least one of her family duties. Her failure to show up at the christening of his three children has left a bleeding wound in Sherborne's side ...well, the sides of both of us. But ~

finally, our sister has realised that she has family obligations.

"As I said, I am overjoyed, and I hope that you will have a pleasant and enjoyable time with her." He pauses. "There is one thing you should know, however … and it gives me great pain to say it: Wilhelmina … how shall I put it in such a way as not to spoil the meeting? Wilhelmina has always had a slender relationship with the truth. Our beloved parents tried to correct the fault, but I am afraid she resisted their efforts. Of course, I was away at school much of the time, so I only saw her in the holidays, but her capacity to make up stories and embellish the facts was one of the reasons I chose to keep her at a distance."

"So, you think I shouldn't believe a word she says?"

"As far as my brother goes, I own, she may have a point. Sherborne was not the best of brothers to her ~ nor to me, I confess. I wish it wasn't so, but I have to face the truth. Had I been in the house, I would have defended her from his tormenting and bullying, but as I said, I was away. I expect you have seen how he treats his own offspring ~ especially the girl. It is very similar to his behaviour when a boy. I have reasoned with him on many occasions, dearest aunt, believe me. I reminded him of the distress our sister suffered at his hands. But he accepts no responsibility. I worry about that girl of his."

"She has a name."

"Yes, she does. Poor little Henrietta. So sad. So very sad." Arthur Harbinger casts his eyes down to the carpet, a picture of regret.

Men, Euphemia Harbinger thinks to herself. They think they are being so clever, but in reality, they are so transparent you could use them as window-glass. She sits on in silence, willing her glassy nephew to get up and leave.

"I regret having to be the bearer of such information, dearest aunt," Arthur says finally, lifting his head with a sigh. "But it is best you know the lie of the land, as it were. Now, I see you are tired. I shall leave you to rest. Please give dear sister Wilhelmina my warmest wishes. We were always close as children."

"Even though you were away at school most of the time?" the old woman puts in slyly.

He is not fazed. "Oh, school could not divide two such fond children. She may have forgotten, over time, how we played together, but the memories are imprinted upon my heart."

He rises, gives her a polite bow, and is shown out by the housekeeper. Harbinger swings his cane jauntily as he heads for the nearest cab rank. He has done some good there, he thinks. The old fool might be bamboozled by sister Wilhelmina and whatever mad tales she chooses to relate; she might even be persuaded to leave her a little something in her Will, but, with a bit of luck, it will come from Sherborne's portion, not his. He has prepared the ground nicely and sown the seeds of doubt in his aunt's mind. He saw it clearly on her face. Let his sister come now ~ he has queered her pitch. Job done and done well.

****

Evening gently falls. Harriet stands on a wooden chair by an open window, watching the black angles of the rooftops, and the bright stars between. Increments of light and shadow cross the floor. The attic room she has commandeered for her current living quarters has a bed, a washstand and a small rickety wooden table. It was clearly a maid's room, at a time when the house had more occupants and numerous servants. There is even a spotlessly clean chamber-pot under the bed. Now, the only resident servant is the living-in housekeeper, and she sleeps in a first-floor bedroom, to be on hand if needed in the night.

On the small table are the remains of Harriet's supper: fragments of soft white bread, a pot of strawberry jam, a pitcher of lemonade and some cake crumbs, all filched from the larder while nobody was around. Being a ghost is very much easier than she thought.

The darkness shifts and wanes. The streets below are peopled with shades. In Harriet's imagination, they are joined by the ghosts of the past, who lived and died and now hang about the city. Dragging their slinking shadows, they stand at doors and crave admittance.

****

There is nothing like a nice juicy pie, into which a well-manicured parliamentary finger can be inserted. Here is the Honourable Thomas Langland, MP, seated at a table in a private room in his Gentleman's Club. The table is laid for two. The silverware gleams, the linen is starched, the crystal glasses glint in the overhead light.

Langland is entertaining a business acquaintance, namely, Wm. Boxworth ~ aka William Wilberforce Wilkins Boxworth, a squat, wide-mouthed, small-eyed, unscrupulous, moral-free property developer. People meeting Boxworth for the first time are invariably reminded of a species of unpleasant and venomous toad. The effect is heightened by his pockmarked face and croaky voice.

Plates of beefsteak and kidney pudding have been served and are being consumed, despite the heat of the day. Boxworth is a formidable trencherman, shovelling food into his mouth and splashing gravy liberally onto the spotless white linen tablecloth. His companion picks at his meal and regards his guest with fastidious distaste.

Eventually, having scraped his plate clean with his knife, and wiped his mouth on a napkin, Boxworth sighs, stifles a burp, leans back and undoes a couple of waistcoat buttons on his loud check suit. "Well, Langland, that was a fine meal, that was. Sets a man up for the afternoon, a good dinner like that."

Langland, who has long discarded the concept of a midday dinner for the more refined term luncheon, inclines his head accommodatingly. "Shall we order coffee and brandy?" he asks. "We have much to discuss."

He raises a hand, and beckons to one of the hovering-at-a-discreet-distance club staff. A quiet word, and the man glides out of the room, returning a short while later. The silver tray is set down, and the fragrant brew poured from a silver coffee pot into the small porcelain cups, which are placed alongside the balloon-shaped brandy glasses. Langland gets out his gold monogrammed cigar case.

"I trust everything is in place?" he says, proffering the case to his guest.

Boxworth helps himself, then stirs his coffee vigorously. "The room is booked at the George Hotel. Posters and flyers distributed, and advertisements have been placed in all the best newspapers. I told you, Langland, if I embark on an enterprise, it is done properly. As you very well know, eh? And when it is an enterprise that's going to make me a very rich man, it is done even more properly … eh? … eh? … haw, haw, haw!"

Langland smiles thinly. Truth to tell, he finds the companionship of Wm. Boxworth not to his taste. The man has absolutely no class. None at all. He'd be embarrassed to introduce him to any of his county set, or to be seen with him socially. But his prowess in the field of speculative enterprises is second to none. A rough diamond, with the emphasis on rough. He has the same ruthless streak as Langland possesses. He also has the gift of the gab, a useful trick for spiriting money out of investors' pockets. Langland himself has already backed him on several speculative and barely legal building projects ~ for which he has received a good return for his initial outlay.

This, however, is to be the biggest enterprise yet. Langland has already played his part: he has used his influence to get parliamentary authority for a scheme to build a railway line to bring travellers into the City from one of the newly built suburbs. Of course, such an undertaking requires vast amounts of money, to be raised by offering shares to potential investors in the joint stock company, which is what the morrow's meeting is about.

The public mania for investing in railway shares is at its frenetic height. Millions of pounds have been put into the various underground and overhead railway companies, the ornate stations that serve them and the vast hotels that hover nearby, making their shareholders large fortunes. It is even rumoured that Queen Victoria herself has bought shares in one company (according to *Punch* magazine).

"Trust me, Langland," Boxworth grins, showing a row of grey tombstone teeth, "once the public sees the brochures and hears about the opportunities for making money, nothing will stop them. We'll have to hold them back, I can tell you right now. The Boxland Joint Stock Railway Company is going to make us both very, very wealthy men. Your name fronting it, my business ability building it, we can't lose!

"But this time, there'll be no … little difficulties, eh?" Boxworth continues, puffing cigar smoke rings at the painted ceiling. "No last minute hiccups. No third parties poking their noses in. No midnight escapades. I tell you straight, Langland, you'll be on your own if there are, coz I'm not going to save your reputation again. Pulled your irons out of the fire last time and a pretty risky operation it was. Once was quite enough."

The Honourable MP sits a little more upright. "I can assure you, Boxworth, nothing of that sort will happen again this time." he says stiffly.

"Good show," the speculator nods. He tosses back the last of his brandy, then levers himself out of his seat. "Right then, I'll be off. Thanks for the dinner, Langland. Appreciated, as always, and I'll see you tomorrow morning at the meeting."

He rolls towards the door, waving a fat hand as he departs. Langland watches him, anger hardening his face. Bad enough that he has to deal with this man, but that he should threaten him ~ *him*? It is not to be tolerated. Without his patronage and liberal string-pulling, Boxworth would be nothing. A small-time speculative builder living in a dingy backstreet, instead of a fine new house in Chalk Farm. That was the trouble with the lower classes. You give them the benefit of your patronage, you haul them out of the gutter they are squatting in, you do them innumerable favours, you make them what they are today, and as a result, they decide they are now as good as you.

Langland sits on, brooding. Eventually, he stubs out the cigar and calls for his hat and stick. He has no committee meetings scheduled, nor is he down to speak in the House. He has one important appointment he must keep, though. It is said you can't con a con man. Langland is about to test that theory out to its fullest extent. He hauls his watch out of his waistcoat pocket and asks the doorman to whistle him up a cab.

A short while later, the Honourable Thomas Langland, MP arrives back at his parliamentary office. Instructing the clerk, whose name he still cannot remember, that he is expecting a visitor and when the man arrives, he is to be shown straight through, he then busies himself with re-arranging the letters on his desk, none of which will be read, as he has far better things to focus on than the woes and worries of his constituents.

Eventually, the visitor is announced. Langland rises from behind the desk, his face wreathed in a smile of welcome. He settles the visitor in one of the chairs, calls for coffee (which is refused), then returns to his own seat, resting his chin on his hands and waits, expectantly. It is a technique he has honed over the years. Always wait for the prey to actually enter the trap before striking.

Arthur Harbinger (for it is he) clears his throat importantly, and removes his gloves, placing them carefully on the arm of his chair. Then he opens his briefcase and takes out a brochure. "Well, Langland, I have studied the information you so kindly sent me," he says, "and I am extremely impressed by your proposal, I have to say. I have always taken an interest in the growth of the railway business. Those who got in right at the start have made fortunes, have they not?"

Langland agrees. They have indeed. He, amongst them.

"So, I am honoured to be invited to be an early investor in your new enterprise," Harbinger goes on. "How many shares are you offering?"

Langland pretends to consider this carefully. "We have received many inquiries already," he says, studying the far wall intently. "A new railway company is always of great interest, as you say, and despite trying to keep the news private, alas, it has leaked out, as these things do. There will be a public meeting held tomorrow, as you know, at which people of independent financial means can come, listen to the proposal, and then invest as they see fit.

"I am, however, in the fortunate position of being able to offer you a chance to secure your partnership in the enterprise before we go public. I consider you a valued friend. I think a total of two hundred and sixty shares would insure you a good stake in the enterprise ~ maybe even a seat on the board? Perhaps you might like to attend our inaugural company meeting tomorrow? What say you? Are you with us?"

The number has been carefully chosen before the visit ~ not too large, not too small. Langland waits for the bait to be taken. He does not have to wait long.

"I am with you every step of the way, or should I say, every inch of track?" Harbinger laughs, leaning eagerly forward in his seat. "Now, let us get down to brass tacks. I am keen to have as much of a stake in the Boxland Joint Stock Railway Company as I possibly can."

And it is as easy as that.

Sometime later, Arthur Harbinger emerges into the sunshine, having agreed the sum that will guarantee him a major share in the Boxland Joint Stock Railway Company and give him a seat on the board as one of the directors. It is a great deal more money than he intended to part with. He feels lightheaded with excitement. He is on the board of a brand-new railway company! His name will appear at the head of any correspondence. He will attend shareholders' meetings and pocket dividends galore. One in the eye for his little brother, he thinks. He cannot wait to parade his good fortune in front of him.

Harbinger walks to the nearest cab stand and directs the driver to take him to his bank. He is going to have to arrange to borrow some money, on a very temporary basis of course, to fund his contribution to the proposed enterprise, as he does not currently have nearly enough in his bank account to back the cheque. A short-term bridging-loan. But he will be able to pay it back, he reminds himself, just as soon as his wretched Aunt Euphemia shuffles off to the next life.

Meanwhile, Thomas Langland makes a careful note of the conversation that has just taken place, and places it in the Boxland folder on his desk, for future reference. No paperwork has changed hands, of course; the deal has been done on a handshake between two gentlemen, whose word is as good as their bond. Especially when one of them is an Honourable Member of Parliament.

Let us now follow Arthur Harbinger as he makes his way to Carson & Stevens private bank in Threadneedle Street. It is one of many private banking concerns in the City of London. He enters the impressive portals. Here are sombre-suited clerks behind wooden partitions, their heads bent over their day-books as they add and subtract, cast-up accounts and weigh out gold and silver, which they transfer with their small brass shovels over the counter to their waiting customers.

Harbinger is approached by one of the senior clerks, who conducts him into the dark-panelled inner sanctum, where Mr Carson, a noble-featured man with silver hair, who is clad in an old-fashioned black frock coat and spotless white cravat, rises from behind his desk and welcomes him with a warm smile and an extended hand of ritual greeting, for both men are members of the same Lodge. Harbinger has banked here since the bank itself was formed, thus Carson & Stevens are the beneficiaries of many years of reputable business transactions. And a few slightly less reputable.

"Please be seated, Mr Harbinger," Carson says. "How are things in the great world of insurance?"

"Oh, fine, as always," Harbinger says, carefully smoothing out the creases in his trousers. "So profitable, in fact, that I have come to request a small short-term loan to invest in an enterprise that I expect to make me a very healthy profit."

The banker steeples his fingers under his chiselled chin and leans forward, an inquiring expression upon his face.

"I have recently become a shareholder in the Boxland Joint Stock Railway Company," Harbinger says. "Here is a copy of the brochure. You will see that an MP of impeachable pedigree and integrity is one of the joint founders of the company."

"I do see that, and I congratulate you."

Harbinger looks down modestly. "Thank you. Now, here is my quandary. I have pledged an initial sum of forty thousand pound against the success of the enterprise. If the bank could see its way to advancing me the money, it would secure the immediate future of the company and enable us to move forward at pace. I would, naturally, use my own contacts to make sure that the bank increased its customers and investors as a result. I flatter myself that I am not without influence in various fields of business and elsewhere. And I am on the cusp of acquiring a large amount of money from the Will of a close relative."

"It is a very large sum of money indeed, Mr Harbinger. Let me study the brochure," the banker says. "In my position as head of this bank, every business-like precaution has to be taken. I have my own shareholders' interests to consider."

"Of course. Please take as long as you wish. I am entirely at your disposal," Harbinger says, staring at the opposite wall with an expression of polite concern. He is pretty sure this is a formality. The money will be forthcoming. The opportunity is too enticingly tempting. "We, the shareholders of the company, will repay you with whatever rate you think right to charge," he adds.

The banker reads. The clock ticks. Harbinger allows his mind to dwell upon the glorious future and how he intends to spend it. After a decent interval, the banker raises his head and nods. Harbinger rises, effusively expressing his gratitude. They shake hands again. Then the banker calls for his cashier and orders him to pay over forty thousand-pound notes.

Harbinger walks out of the bank, the banknotes folded and hidden, and turns his footsteps towards the West End. Warm rain is steadily falling. He hails a cab and tells the driver to take him to his Club. It is time to celebrate. Beyond the cab's windows, the streets glitter with rain. If he half-closes his eyes, he sees not raindrops but golden guineas tumbling from the sky.

****

Next morning, bright and early, a police sergeant from Marylebone Police Office arrives at the Excelsior Hotel to take some more details from the Harbinger family. Contrary to hopes and expectations, Harriet has still not turned up, but on the positive side, there have been no bodies found overnight that answer to her description.

As his wife remains prostrate with grief, Sherborne is forced to deal with the sergeant alone. Woodenly, he supplies the details requested, realising, as his memory strains to answer the officer, that he is barely able to recall such details as the colour of his daughter's eyes or whether she had any distinguishing marks on her body. Let alone what she was wearing when she went missing. Clothes, he presumes, but that is about as far as he can go.

It is as if Harriet has lived amongst them, but almost invisibly. And now she has gone, leaving only a feeling of anger that her foolish and reckless actions have caused him so many problems. His anger grows exponentially when the door to the hotel's smoking room unexpectedly opens to admit his brother Arthur, whose eyes widen in astonishment upon seeing a uniformed policeman in close consultation with his younger brother.

"Hulloo … what is up?" he asks, approaching them.

Sherborne hastily closes down the interview, promising the police officer he will await any news. As soon as the sergeant has left, Arthur drags over an armchair and sits down, leaning forward, his lean features alight with interest.

"Well, well, brother Sherborne ~ this is a sight I did not expect to see. I came hoping to hear you had come up with a plan to thwart our little sister and secure our inheritance. And now I find you being questioned by the constabulary. What crime have you committed, eh? I hope it has nothing to do with our aunt ~ don't tell me you have made use of her pillow!"

Sherborne clenches his teeth in annoyance. "Harriet has gone missing," he tells Arthur. "I told Charlotte from the start that it was a mistake to bring her to London. I said she'd be better off staying in the house with the governess, but she whined and wheedled. Said she wanted to make sure the blasted parrot didn't come to any harm. And now she's disappeared from the hotel, and God knows where she's gone."

Arthur Harbinger stares at him, a pitying expression on his face. Just as he did when they were youngsters, and his brother had done something idiotic, for which he would suffer later on, when it was related, in great detail, to their father. As it always was.

"Oh, I think we can do better than the Deity," Arthur smiles thinly. "You mentioned the parrot? Use your brain, little brother. Where is the bird? Yes ~ I see you follow me. The girl has gone around to our aunt's house to play with it."

Sherborne stares at him. "She has?"

"Of course. If you don't believe me, go there yourself. You said she and the old fool got on like a house on fire? That's where you'll find her."

Sherborne leaps to his feet. "Damn it ~ you could be right," he exclaims. "I'll get my hat and fetch her straight back here. And then won't she be in trouble!"

Arthur Harbinger waves his hand at the vacated chair. "Sit ye back down, Sherborne. Not so fast. Take a breath and THINK, for once in your life. Who's coming to pay a morning call on the old nuisance, maybe even today? Sister Wilhelmina. Now, we have both been told we are not welcome when she visits, but if we had someone already in the house who could report back to us, wouldn't that be a good thing?"

Sherborne's mouth drops open. "You are right again. Why didn't I think of it?"

Because you are a very stupid man and I am always superior to you, Arthur thinks, but doesn't say. "Listen to me now: I propose calling off the hunt. Tell the police to stop looking. We know where the girl is. In a few days, you can call round, 'distraught' and collect her. Then she can tell us what went on at the meeting."

Sherborne's face is that of a small boy who has suddenly realised it is his birthday. "But this is wonderful! Harriet is bound to be introduced to Wilhelmina and allowed to sit in the corner while the adults talk."

"Exactly. You have it in one."

Sherborne claps his long bony hands together. "I shall go and tell Charlotte at once," he says. "You have put my mind at rest. Thank you, Arthur."

"Just let me know when you have collected the girl from the house. I'd like to hear what she has to say."

"I shall. I certainly shall," Sherborne's face is wreathed in a smile.

"Well, as you no longer have to come up with a plan, thanks to the precipitate but fortunate actions of the girl, I shall be on my way. I have a very important meeting to attend in my new role as the director of a railway company." He pauses long enough to allow the words to sink in and to see the envy in his brother's face, before turning his back on him and walking briskly away.

Arthur Harbinger heads for the George Hotel. Of course, what he didn't say to his brother was that he might be quite wrong, and the girl could be lying in some sordid alleyway with her throat cut. But then, his brother has two other children, so one less would hardly matter, in the great scheme of things.

****

The inaugural meeting of the Boxland Joint Stock Railway Company is about to get under way. Here is Thomas Langland, MP, clad in his expensive hand-tailored suit, his shiniest beaver hat and linen so white and starched that it dazzles the eye. He sits on a raised dais in the large meeting room of the George Hotel. Next to him (if we are going down the social scale), sits the brand-new chief shareholder Arthur Harbinger, who, a short while earlier, has handed over his contribution to the proposed enterprise, and at the far end (in so many ways) sits Wm. Boxworth in his loudest check suit, a paisley cravat and unmatching striped waistcoat. He puffs away at a big cigar and smiles in a reptilian fashion.

At the back of the room, hotel staff in black and white uniforms discreetly arrange cups, bring in urns and set out china plates, because if you are going to extract money from the great British public, it is always a good idea to include free tea and biscuits. Along one side of the room are tables, behind which sit smartly dressed young clerks with ledgers and cash boxes, ready to sign up prospective shareholders and relieve them of their money. The whole set-up looks very professional and business-like, except that the clerks are rented, and being paid by the hour, and after today, will never be seen again.

Meanwhile, prospective punters are lining up outside the hotel, jostling for space with anti-railway protestors carrying placards with slogans such as: **'Trains Kill!'**, **'SAVE THE HORSE & CARRIAGE'**, and **'Railways are the Spawn of Satan'**, though nobody is taking any notice of them. The prospect of buying shares in another great British railway enterprise is all they are focused upon. The crowd is abuzz as the doors open and they stream in to find their seats.

Once all are seated, and the excess has been placed in an overflow area at the back, Langland rises to his feet. An expectant hush descends, except for one deaf old lady who continues talking loudly to her companion, until shushed by those around her.

Langland favours the audience with a winning smile ~ the one that got him elected to a safe parliamentary seat and will probably keep him sitting there until the end of his political career, from whence he will transfer seamlessly to a seat on the board of some city bank. When he is sure all eyes are fixed upon him, he welcomes everybody, introduces himself (modestly) and his two fellow directors.

He reminds his listeners of the greatness of the land to which they all belong, the innumerable benefits, the fantastic achievements in science, in engineering, in industry. How proud he is to call himself a British citizen, part of the greatest country on earth, respected and revered all over the world, with an Empire that reflects back the light of sovereignty and democracy.

It is, with a few tweaks here and there, the maiden speech he gave when he was first elected many years ago. Not that they know this, of course. Langland speaks of the wonders of the modern railway, and delicately hints at the fortunes made by those who bought shares in the early companies. He reminds the audience that Queen Victoria herself has bought shares in a railway company, managing, without saying it directly, to hint that it might be this one.

He speaks eloquently, but not for too long. After all, he is not the main attraction here ~ the main attraction is harrumphing and fidgeting in his seat at the end of the row. Eventually, Langland makes the necessary introduction, and sits down, leaving the floor to Wm. Boxworth.

It is the first time Arthur Harbinger, who is technically only invited for pecuniary reasons, and to make up the numbers, has met Boxworth. He has never encountered the 'rough and ready, man of the people, rags to riches, boosterish,' style of oratory employed by the developer. He listens in amazement, unable to take his eyes off the bulky Boxworth, who holds his audience in the same way a circus barker might. Langland, who has not only encountered it, but regards it with deep disdain, studies his well-manicured nails and thinks about how many racehorses he will buy with the money.

Eventually, Boxworth boasts himself to a halt. The invitation to buy shares is made and to the three men's delight, the tables where the clerks wait are quickly overwhelmed by punters waving fistfuls of notes, while their wives retire to the back of the room, where they help themselves to tea. Small groups of ladies quickly form, based on certain sartorial signals unknown to the outside male. Langland glances at the clerks, the lines of eager punters, nods in satisfaction, then steps down from the dais and prepares to do what he does best, meeting and greeting the general public.

Harbinger watches with some envy as the smooth-talking Member of Parliament works the room, occasionally signalling out an individual for a favoured word, placing a hand on the shoulder of another. It is clear that he has invited some of his own close parliamentary friends to the event. It is also clear that Langland is a much liked and trusted person. He has the happy knack of pleasing people. Harbinger, on the other hand, does not. His own particular area of expertise lies elsewhere: worrying people into taking out life insurance for themselves and their nearest and dearest.

He wonders fleetingly whether he should descend into the throng and attempt to be pleasant to complete strangers. But as he does not think any of the assembled company would be interested in purchasing life insurance, and that is the only basis upon which he would care to exchange conversation, he decides to remain where he is. As for the ladies at the back, their bright bonnets dipping and rising, their teacups tinkling, their womanish laughter hovering lightly on the air ~ a shudder goes through him. He'd rather face a cageful of monkeys than advance upon the gay throng by the refreshment tables.

Arthur Harbinger lets his gaze stray towards the far end of the meeting room, where various unlikely people are attempting to enter (including some of the banner wavers). He feels completely out of his depth. Why, even the uncouth Wm. Boxworth is paying court to a pair of equally impossibly clad fellow roughnecks. Their loud vulgar laughter falls like grated glass upon his sensitive ear. He feels revulsion rising up within him. He has done his duty, and that is enough. He crams on his hat and heads for the door, pushing past the waifs and strays on his way out.

****

Meanwhile, Harriet Harbinger, who has strayed, but is not in the least waif-like, is settling into her new life as a ghost. In a house peopled by an invalid, one housekeeper, a part-time maid and cook, it is surprising how easy it is to avoid detection. Food is left on sideboards or sits on trays outside the green baize door leading to the basement kitchen, just waiting for her to help herself. Her great aunt eats like a bird, but still expects the full range of breakfast meats to tempt her waning palate. Harriet is happy to help her out with the surplus.

After breakfast, while morning ablutions and dressing the invalid are taking place, she slides into the sitting room and plays with the parrot, who is delighted to see her. After this, she retires to her attic quarters to read and study. Harriet has discovered a room containing shelves of books. More books than she has ever seen in her life. She has paged through a couple of novels (she is not allowed to read novels at home, as they are supposed to be 'fast' and bad for young girls' brains), eventually helping herself to an atlas and a big fat book of history and world facts, which she has taken up to the attic. With such riches, and her own fertile story-telling imagination, she can occupy herself for hours.

Luncheon follows the same pattern as breakfast: random but sufficient. Then, while her great aunt takes a nap in her room, and the servants are busy elsewhere, Harriet is free to wander around, looking at the ornaments and mementos of Euphemia Harbinger's past, though she always keeps an ear open for a servant's footsteps, ready to duck behind a curtain or a door, or hide under a table.

In the evening, when the house has settled into quiet, Harriet tiptoes down the stairs, helps herself to whatever she can find in the well-stocked larder. Then she slides the bolt of the kitchen door and takes her supper out into the small basement area to eat. High above her, the moon is a luminous disc on a cloth of black velvet; pinprick stars shine silverly bright. She maps the planets by the light of a streetlamp, picking out constellations from one of the star charts in her book.

All the while, up in the street the night-time people pass to and fro. She hears their footsteps, snatches of conversation, arguments, whispers, and sometimes, as night wears on, loud singing and arguments. Night-time cabs clop by. Cats howl and prowl. Dogs bark. Small animals scurry. In the distance, the local church bell tolls the hour, then the quarter, half, and three-quarter hour. Nobody notices the slight figure sitting on the stone step under the arch of night sky, with her supper and her book on her lap.

For the first time in her short life, Harriet is blissfully happy. Gone is the aura of fear that always surrounded her father's arrival back from work. Harriet didn't even need to hear the front door being closed; she knew he was back by the stillness in the air. The very hallway seemed to hold its breath. If such a place as heaven on earth exists, Harriet is inhabiting it now. And thus, time passes by, as if in a beautiful dream. But like all dreams, it cannot last. Eventually, one has to wake up.

The morning of the third day arrives. Harriet has now learned the routines of the house. She waits at the top of the stairs until the breakfast tray has been removed, and the old lady helped up to her bedroom to be dressed. Then, with silent catlike tread, she scurries down and helps herself to cold toast, a few rashers of bacon and a cup of milk from the tray.

With breakfast in her possession, Harriet returns to her attic domain, tucks herself back in bed and opens one of her books. Munching her breakfast while reading about the skeletal structures of Australian mammals keeps her occupied for some time. Eventually, she sets the book aside and gets ready for the day, a process that involves splashing her face with cold water, buttoning herself into her very crumpled dress and running her fingers through her matted hair.

Harriet tiptoes out of her room onto the landing. Today her plan is to sneak downstairs and, after playing with the parrot, slide open the catch on the small side window. With a bit of luck, she might manage a few hours outside, exploring the neighbourhood. She stands in the hallway, ears strained. Muffled voices from the first floor indicate that the owner of the house is still being made ready for the day.

Harriet hurries into the sitting room, where she is greeted by the grey parrot, who turns somersaults on his perch at the sight of her. She checks his food cup and his water, then lets him nibble her fingers through the bars, while she croons songs to him. Hearing voices in the passageway, Harriet darts across the room and slips between the folding doors that separate the sitting room from the drawing room.

She peers through the crack and sees Great Aunt Euphemia in a violet silk dress and smart lace cap being seated gently on the sofa by Rose. The parrot screeches *"Harriet ... hello, Harriet! Where are you?"* and the old woman smiles at it indulgently.

"No, Poll, Harriet is not coming today. But we are having a visitor, an important one, whom I have waited some time to see, so you'd better be on your best behaviour!"

Harriet sucks in her breath as the front doorbell sounds, and Rose leaves the room. A short while later, she returns. "If you please, Miss Harbinger, Miss Wilhelmina Harbinger to see you."

Harriet gently widens the gap in the folding door, so that she can spy on the visitor. She sees a slim young woman, her face half-hidden by the brim of a straw bonnet, trimmed in blue ribbon rosettes. Her dark hair ~ the same colour as Harriet's own, is parted at the front and tucked up under the bonnet at the sides. She wears a pale green dress, buttoned high at the neck, and an ivory shawl with long fringes. Harriet tries to make out her features but all she can really see is a pair of spectacles, perched on a short sharp nose.

"Sit down, Wilhelmina," Euphemia Harbinger says. "I am pleased to see you after all this time. Tea will be served shortly. I hope you have had a reasonable journey. I find this heat very oppressive."

"Indeed, it is," the young woman replies, her voice low and pleasantly musical in tone. "But the park is refreshing and green, and I enjoy seeing nature at work and play."

"You visit London for the first time?"

"It is a wonderful city."

"Really? Do you think so? I have to say that I find it too loud, and too dusty. And there are far too many people," the old woman replies. "But then, I am old. I daresay when I was your age, I'd find it amusing enough. Though I have always held Paris to be a much finer city. Now, you will take tea? Cook has made some shortbread, I see. I seem to remember you always had a sweet tooth as a child."

Wilhelmina Harbinger accepts a cup from Rose and helps herself to a biscuit. The small ghost mentally crosses her fingers that there will be a few biscuits left over after the visit ends. The conversation meanders politely through the weather, the state of the streets, the problem finding good fruit and fresh milk in high

143

summer, the cost of cotton gloves. Harriet's concentration falters. She is about to return to her books when she hears great aunt say, suddenly and briskly:

"Well, enough small talk. Let us not beat about the bush any longer, Wilhelmina. I wanted to see you before I die because there is something I do not understand, and I wish to have it explained to me. When your father passed away, I was led to believe that everything left was to be shared equally between you and your two brothers. And yet, you tell me in your letter that you have received nothing at all, and moreover, that you have had to work ever since to earn your living and support yourself. Is this the truth?"

The young woman sighs. "It is quite true, dear aunt. I was excluded from the reading of the Will, and then told by my brothers that our father had left everything to Arthur and Sherborne. You must understand that my brothers and I were not on good terms ~ we fell out many years ago, when we were still children. They looked down on me because I was a girl, and my father always favoured them over me ~ I do not complain, I merely state the facts."

"I see. I recall visiting your house when you were a little girl. You had a white kitten you doted on ~ what was its name? You dressed it in dolls clothes and wheeled it round in a pram, I remember that quite clearly."

"Blanche. How strange that you remember that! My brother Sherborne locked her in the coal shed."

"An unkind thing to do."

Wilhelmina's mouth tightens. "He was not a kind child. Neither of them was ever kind."

There is a pause. Harriet tilts her head to see what is going on in the room. Both women are staring hard at each other. They are not speaking, but a conversation is clearly happening, even though no words are being uttered. The silence fills the room so thickly it could almost be cut into slices and served up on a plate.

"I should not like to die knowing any member of my family has had to struggle through life, when it is in my power to make amends," Euphemia Harbinger says slowly.

"You need not worry, dear aunt. I am employed. I have a profession that I love, and I earn money for doing it. I may not live as well as my brothers do, nor in such luxury, but I survive. And I am content. I owe no man my duty or obedience. Nor their praise. It is important for a modern woman to be independent and not rely on anyone else. At least, that is what I think. As the poetess writes: *'And in that we have nobly striven at least. Deal with us nobly, woman that we be. And honour us with truth, if not with praise.'* You may not be familiar with her work."

"Hmm. Yes, I have read *Aurora Leigh*. Many years ago, of course. And I am familiar with the work of Mary Wollstonecraft also. Well, you may be right, my dear. It's a new world and I am glad to see you are making your own way in it. Nevertheless, I would like to leave you something in my Will to make up for what you ought, by rights, to have had. That is why I wished to see you. Some reparation should be made, and I am rich enough to do it and would like to do it. What do you say?"

There is a pause. Harriet leans her ear to the crack in the door. Finally, Wilhelmina Harbinger replies, "I say, thank you, dear aunt, that is indeed most generous, but no. I should not like to fall under money's spell and become greedy and grasping and uncaring like ..." she lets the words fade into silence.

Another meaningful pause. Then the old lady rings the little bell on the arm of the chair, and Rose enters. "Bring me my jewel case," she orders.

The housekeeper goes, returning shortly with a large green shantung case, which she places on the sofa beside her mistress. The old lady unclips the tiny gold clasp and lifts out tray after tray of bright jewels.

"Then maybe you might accept some jewellery? I have beautiful diamonds, given to me in my youth by an admirer. And this ruby ring is worth a small fortune."

"That, too, is most kind, dear aunt, but I am not permitted to wear jewels in my current employment," comes the calm reply. "However, I should be glad of a keepsake, to remember you by."

The old lady beckons to her. "Then choose whatever you want, Wilhelmina."

The young woman's hand passes over the sparkling brooches, necklaces, and rings. "I'd like to have this, if I may," she says.

"The forget-me-not brooch? Ah, that was given to me by a famous artist when I sat for him. I was about your age at the time. A good choice. You are sure that is all?"

Wilhelmina nods. "Yes, this is perfect. And now I must go. It was such a pleasure to call on you after all this time, dear aunt. And thank you for my keepsake. It will always remind me of you, and of this meeting."

She stands. The old lady rings the bell and asks Rose to show the visitor out. After she has left the room, Euphemia Harbinger starts putting jewellery back into the box, but her hands soon fall into her lap and lie still. Next minute, soft snores fill the air. Emboldened, Harriet slips through the partition, approaches the sofa, and stands staring down at the jewels. She has never seen so many sparkling things. Her mother has a small necklace of seed pearls and a silver cross on a chain for Sundays, but that is all.

Harriet lifts up a diamond bracelet, fascinated by the way it catches the light, then releases it, brighter than before. It is as if it has swallowed the sun and is throwing

146

out rainbows, she thinks. The beauty of it grabs hold of something inside her and tears it open. All at once, she cannot breathe. She is so engrossed in the sensation that she fails to notice the parlour door quietly opening, fails to hear the soft footsteps of the housekeeper crossing the carpet, fails to feel her presence just behind her, until Rose's hand suddenly grasps her shoulder, and then it is too late.

"Harriet?" the parrot squawks, as she is hauled unceremoniously out of the room, *"Harriet ~ go up to your room at once, you stupid girl!"*

Harriet Harbinger is maid-handled down to the kitchen and plonked unceremoniously onto a wooden stool. Rose goes to stand by the Welsh dresser, her arms folded, her expression stern. A black and white pillar. Harriet bites her lip. She is certainly in trouble, though she is not exactly sure how much trouble she is actually in.

"I'm waiting, young miss."

"I … it … I wanted to see my parrot," Harriet tells her.

"How did you get into the house?"

"Window."

"How long have you been here?"

Harriet bites her lip. "A few days."

"Does your father know you are here?"

Harriet studies her nails. There is a semi-circle of dirt under each one.

"I see," Rose says sternly. "Well, that explains the missing food, and the sounds I have heard up in the attic. It was you. I thought, at first, that we had rats. I was going to send for the ratcatcher. Don't you know that my mistress is unwell? Her heart is failing. Seeing you standing over her unexpectedly like that could have brought on a heart attack and killed her. Now, what do you have to say for yourself?"

A lone tear trickles down Harriet's cheek. "I didn't know. I am sorry. So sorry."

Rose's expression unhardens slightly. "Well, no harm was done, fortunately. But your parents must be out of their minds with worry. London isn't a safe city for a little girl to go wandering about in. I shall take you back to your hotel at once, and you can explain to your parents where you have been. Come, we shall go now, while my mistress sleeps."

Harriet shifts on the stool. "Might I … I need to …"

Rose rolls her eyes. "Upstairs on the first floor. And be quick."

Harriet runs straight up to her attic hideaway and grabs her precious notebook and pencil, thrusting them into the pocket of her pinafore. She takes a final look round, mentally bidding farewell to the books, the view from the window, and her freedom. Then she descends to the kitchen and follows the housekeeper out of the basement door, and up into the street.

They set off for the Excelsior Hotel. Harriet tries to walk as slowly as she can, but Rose is in no mood to let her dally and chivvies her along until they reach the hotel entrance and the liveried doorman, whose eyes widen when he sees them.

"My, you are in such trouble, young lady," he says, shaking his head. "Half the police force in London has been combing the streets night and day trying to find you."

Harriet casts her eyes down, thus missing the wink the doorman exchanges with the housekeeper, who gives her a brisk little push through the door.

"Go and find your parents, Harriet. And please do not attempt to pull any tricks like that again," she says, hurrying off.

Harriet drags herself into the lobby, and hauls herself across it, feeling as if every eye is upon her, and every guest is judging her and finding her wanting. She mounts the stairs to the first floor and knocks on her parents' door.

"Yes? Who is it?" calls her father's voice from within.

A cold feeling of dread steals over her at the sound of it. "It's me, Harriet," she says dully.

There is a second's pause, then the door is flung open, and Harriet is clasped passionately to the maternal bosom. "Oh Harriet, Harriet! How could you run away like that?" sobs her mother, "How could you make us suffer so much? Wicked, wicked girl! To run away from your loving family! What were you thinking?"

Harriet struggles to free herself.

"Now, Charlotte ~ control yourself," her father says. "Remember what we discussed? Harriet, come and stand here. No, here, by the writing desk. Now look me straight in the eye and tell me plainly where you have been hiding for the last three days. And I want the truth. I shall know if you are lying to me, so do not waste my time."

Harriet stares into her father's cold stone-grey eyes. "I have been at great aunt's house," she says in a small voice. "I wanted to see my parrot."

"Aha!" A look of fierce triumph crosses her father's lean face. His features relax into an expression of comprehension.

Harriet does not quite understand it, but decides to capitalise, nevertheless. "I am sorry for what I have done. I did not cause any trouble to great aunt. And I saw my Aunt Wilhelmina while I was there."

Again, her father's eyes light up. To her utter amazement, he smiles at her. "I see. Well, you are back now, and it is almost teatime, so we shall say no more about it, for the present. Go to your room and make yourself presentable ~ you need to change your pinafore and wash your hands before we go down to the dining room. We shall speak about this later."

Harriet stares at him. She had mentally prepared herself for a couple of hard smacks, a deal of hard words and several days on limited rations. Puzzled, she backs out of the room, almost falling over Hanover, who is listening at the keyhole. He glares resentfully at her.

"Why didn't he wallop you one? He's been saying he was going to beat the living daylights out of you when you came back. He was going to break your spirit, he said. My eye ~ were you going to get it!"

Harriet deconstructs this. "Maybe he was just worried about me, and now he's pleased I'm back."

Hanover shakes his head. "No, he's definitely been raging. I heard him. The whole hotel probably heard him. He seemed to change when you told him you'd been at great aunt's house."

"Yes, he did, didn't he?" Harriet agrees thoughtfully. "And when I told him I'd met Aunt Wilhelmina, he actually smiled. Why?"

"What did she look like?" Hanover asks. "Did she talk about father? And the money?"

"Mind your own business," Harriet says tartly.

She runs along the corridor and wrenches open the door to her room. Then, before Hanover can enter and ask any more questions, she turns the key. Harriet lies on her coverlet, staring at the ceiling, thinking things out. She knows she should be feeling guilty, but she does not. Part of this absence of guilt comes from the absence of punishment. An almost unheard-of event. She decides to focus her attention on it.

Gradually, realisation dawns. Her father is not punishing her because she has seen her aunt. He wants to hear what happened. He wants to find out whether Aunt Wilhelmina is going to get a share of the money, and she is the only one who can confirm or deny it. A slow smile spreads across Harriet's face. It is not often that she holds any leverage over her cold unloving parent. So now that she does, she is going to make the most of it.

****

Detective Inspector Stride considers himself to be a fair man. A fair man who does not like to disappoint his colleagues. A fair man who will do whatever it takes to track down a criminal, wherever he may choose to hide. And now, he has failed. He has been unable to track down the murderer of a young parliamentary clerk who had his whole life and career in front of him. He has had to face the man's distraught parents and inform them that his officers, trained detectives at the top of their game, did not have a single clue regarding who had murdered their only son, nor why. That they had explored every avenue and found only dead ends.

So, it is an unhappy detective inspector who makes his way to his favourite lunchtime watering-hole off Fleet Street. Pushing open the door of Sally's Chop House, his nose is assailed with the customary odour of over-boiled cabbage and fatty meat. To his surprise and delight however, he is greeted by the eponymous Sally, who has returned from his holiday. His face is sunburned ~ which is the only difference about him that Stride can spot. His gravy-stained apron looks identical to how it was before he left.

Stride's face brightens. "Good to see you, Sally," he says, making his way to his usual booth at the back.

"And you, Mr Stride," Sally responds, following him at a cautious distance.

The detective might be one of Sally's regulars, but he is not one of his favourite customers, having rather too much the air of policeman about him. If Sally could find a cogent reason to bar Stride, he would. Customers, however innocent, do not like to be reminded of the forces of law and order, especially when they are harmlessly eating their lunch. Stride places his order, then enquires about Sally's holiday.

"Well, you know how it is, Mr Stride," the big man says, mopping down the table with a grey dishcloth. "Once you've seen the sea, you've seen it. I don't go much for this new-fangled sea-bathing lark myself, but the brother and his wife were all for it, so I went along like. Just glad to be back in London. At least the pavements don't crunch and go up and down."

On that elliptical note, Sally goes to fetch Stride's food, leaving his customer to muse on the peculiarity of people. While he is gone, Stride takes a look at one of the newspapers. Sally's patrons favour reading matter at the less intellectually exhausting end of the spectrum, preferring big bold headlines, lots of exclamation marks and short words.

Stride turns the pages listlessly. There are the usual horror stories of giant pigs running riot in the sewers, babies that have grown fins and headless bodies prowling the midnight streets. The corners of the pages are still damp from the licked fingers of previous readers. He consoles himself that, for once, there are no stories, true or false, featuring Scotland Yard and the detective division.

Sally eventually reappears with Stride's plate of chops, gravy and a boiled potato and plonks it down in front of him. "You enjoy your lunch, Mr Stride," he says, retreating to a discreet distance to keep an eye on him, so that the moment Stride sets down his knife and fork, Sally can whisk his plate away, take his money and see him off the premises.

Stride picks at his food morosely for a while. He sighs. Puts his cutlery onto his plate and stares moodily into the middle distance.

"Everythin' to your satisfaction then, Mr Stride?" Sally asks, stepping speedily out of the background into the foreground. "Bit more gravy with that?"

"No, Sally. Thank you. The food is fine. I was musing upon a recent investigation."

"That's orlright then," Sally says.

"I wish it was. I have had to disappoint my colleagues. It does not make for a happy atmosphere."

"That's a shame, then." Sally's experience of staff relations involves shouting at the potboy and nagging the kitchen staff to cut corners.

"It is a great shame, Sally, I agree. Here we had a fine young man, his whole life ahead of him, and I have had to close the investigation on his untimely death as we have no credible witnesses to his demise."

"Can't win 'em all, Mr Stride, is what I say."

"Somebody has got away with murder. That sticks in my craw, Sally. Justice has not been done."

Sally's face is a mask of diplomatically feigned solicitude. In the not-too-distant past, he was a small-time thief of some inadequacy, until he decided to give up a life of crime for a career in catering. The concept of justice evaded is dear to his heart, though never part of his personal experience.

"Nobody who takes another man's life should ever be free to walk the streets," Stride declares, thumping the table with his fist.

"A sentiment wot I totally agrees with, Mr Stride," Sally nods. Taking another man's watch, his umbrella or, in one case, his canteen of cutlery, was a different kettle of fish altogether.

"Justice should be meted out to everyone who breaks the law of this land," Stride continues.

Sally clamps his mouth shut. If there'd been a bit less meting out, he wouldn't have spent quite so much time behind bars for events that were, in his opinion, more a redistribution of wealth than actual larceny.

Stride eats a few more mouthfuls, mops up his gravy with a piece of bread, then places his knife and fork together on his plate. Sally immediately leans over his shoulder and removes it.

"'Nother drink?" he asks solicitously.

Stride shakes his head. He pays for his meal and picks up his hat from the bench.

"I am glad you have returned, Sally. I have missed our little chats."

"So have I, Mr Stride, so have I," the big man lies, accompanying Stride to the door to make sure he leaves. The only good thing about this particular customer, he thinks, as he takes Stride's plate to be sluiced in the bucket of cold water behind the bar, before it is used for someone else, is that he always pays for his food without quibbling and doesn't pocket the eating implements on the way out.

****

Meanwhile, over at the Excelsior Hotel, the Interrogation of Harriet is about to begin. Here are Sherborne Harbinger and his older brother Arthur, seated behind one of the big tables in the deserted dining room, which they have temporarily commandeered. In front of them, standing on a small, tapestried stool, is Harriet herself. The set-up is deliberately designed to be as intimidating and awkward as possible for the young girl.

Arthur Harbinger has actually brought some important looking files with him, which he has opened and spread on the table to add to the gravity of the occasion. It is his intention to make notes of the ensuing interrogation, possibly for use in some profitable capacity in the future. Sherborne is wearing his black business suit. Harriet, in a clean pinafore and frock, eyes them both cautiously, but behind her impassive face, her active mind is already busily at work.

"Now, Harriet," Arthur solemnly says, while folding his arms in as intimidating a manner as he can, "when did you see your Aunt Wilhelmina?"

Harriet remains mute.

"Answer your uncle, Harriet," Sherborne says. He has taken the role of good relative. Temporarily.

"You know when I saw her," Harriet says finally.

"But Uncle Arthur wants to hear it from your own lips, Harriet," says the good relative testily.

Harriet rolls her eyes, mainly because she knows how it irritates her father. "I saw Aunt Wilhelmina at great aunt's house. She was paying a morning call."

"And where were you during this morning call?" Arthur asks.

Harriet gives him a cool stare. "I was in the back parlour, behind the folding doors."

"So, you could see and hear everything that went on?" Sherborne prompts.

Arthur Harbinger raises a warning hand. "Not so fast, brother. One step at a time, if you please. First, we need to find out whether the woman really was Wilhelmina. Now, Harriet, I want you to describe your aunt to us. What did she look like?"

Harriet stares at the far wall, upon which hangs a painting of a fine three-masted Elizabethan galleon breasting a stormy sea. She imagines herself standing on the deck in a tricorne hat, the parrot balancing itself on her shoulder. She has a sword at her belt, and she is riding the waves, captain of her own craft, hearing gulls crying overhead. She has instructed the crew to aim the ship's cannons at her father and uncle.

"I am waiting. Please answer my question, Harriet," says the bad relative, drumming his fingers upon the table.

Harriet gives her crew the order to fire.

"She was very beautiful, with long dark ringlets, and a green silk dress. She had a lovely bonnet with feathers and lots of sparkling rings on her fingers."

Harriet had toyed with portraying her aunt as a fellow pirate but decided that might stretch the credibility gap a bit too far. As it was, she is gratified to see a look of alarm pass between her father and her uncle.

"Rings, you say?" Sherborne queries.

"Sparkling rings?" Arthur adds.

"Oh yes. Lots. I saw them when she took off her gloves. And she arrived in a carriage. I heard the horses. She brought great aunt some lovely presents ~ chocolates and roses. Great aunt was very happy to see her. She said so."

There is a pause while this extremely unwelcome information is processed. Harriet changes the imaginary scenery. Now, her father and uncle are inching along a thin, whippy plank. She is prodding them, cutlass in hand. Beneath them, sharks circle. Waiting.

"Well, brother, this is unexpected. Our sister seems to have come into money after all," Arthur says. "I wonder where she got it from?" He shoots Harriet a stern glance. "I am quite sure that you wouldn't lie to your family, would you, little girl? Lying is against the teaching of God."

Harriet is quite sure that she would. There were so many things her Papa did that were against the teachings of God that a few additions on her part were neither here nor there. And anybody who called her 'little girl' in that dismissive tone of voice deserved to be copiously lied to.

"What did they talk about?" Sherborne asks eagerly.

"Lots of things," Harriet says elliptically.

Arthur Harbinger waves a hand in a go-on motion.

Harriet looks deliberately vague. "Oh, I can't remember everything. I am sorry. They spoke very quietly. But great aunt kept saying: 'No? Did they? Oh, I am so sorry, how very cruel.' And Aunt Wilhelmina said: 'you cannot imagine what I suffered.' She said that several times."

Both brothers wince in fraternal unison and glance away.

"I told you," Arthur hisses under his breath, and Sherborne bites his underlip.

Harriet moves her weight onto her left foot. The sharks, having enjoyed their meal, swim away. "Can I go now?"

Her father glances up. "No, you may not. We have not finished yet," he snaps, good relative morphing suddenly into bad relative. "You have not told us how the meeting ended. Whether great aunt mentioned anything about her Will."

Overnight, in the humid air of her small bedroom, while the rest of the hotel slumbered peacefully, Harriet has been thinking a lot about this. It was a case of creating a set of answers that would be believable, without being so fantastically far-fetched that it threw everything else she said into doubt.

"Well," she begins, taking a deep breath. "I *think* I heard great aunt say something about how she planned to make it up to Aunt Wilhelmina for all the terrible things that had happened to her when she was growing up. And then she showed her a big green box of jewellery and asked her to choose some to take with her for the time being, as a keepsake."

A low groan emits from Arthur Harbinger. He covers his face with his hands.

"And Aunt Wilhelmina said, 'thank you very much', and put a diamond necklace and a diamond bracelet on. Then she put more jewellery into her bag. And great aunt said she could have the rest after she died. And then she said goodbye. That was all I saw. And then the housekeeper found me and brought me back here. Can I go now?"

"Yes, go, go," Sherborne waves her away.

Relief carries Harriet to the door, where she pauses, listening intently. She hears her uncle saying furiously, "The little swine has slipped in behind our backs. I cannot believe it! I will not tolerate it, Sherborne. We are going to have to move fast to rectify this. I blame you. If you hadn't been so determined to cut her out of father's Will, and then lose her address, we might have been able to stop her."

"I?" her father snarls, "I was the one who suggested we gave her a small amount of money as a token gesture, to keep her sweet. This entire mess is your fault. I had high hopes that Charlotte would inherit the jewellery. The diamonds! The diamonds have been filched by our sister! They are reputedly worth a small fortune by themselves. The story always was that aunt was given them by some royal personage."

"YOU expected the diamonds? Really? I am the older brother. The diamonds and the rest of the jewels should, by rights, go to me."

"I don't see why they should. It's not as if you have a wife, or any other female dependants. I have two."

"Oh really? And your wife mixes in the sort of circles where women wear priceless diamonds, does she? Or will she wear them to do the family washing?"

"How dare you impugn my wife, you scoundrel!" Sherborne shouts, jumping out of his seat and squaring up to his brother, fists raised.

Arthur Harbinger follows suit. Harriet, still paused on the threshold, waits wide-eyed and agog to see what will happen next. Alas, just at the moment when fisticuffs seem destined to break out, a waiter comes in with a tray of cups and saucers. Both brothers instantly lower their hands, sink sheepishly into their chairs, and Harriet hurries away.

She returns to her hotel room. It is small, and the view from the window is of the back yard of the building opposite, which seems to be some sort of warehouse. There is a dog tied up, who barks and sometimes cries. She tries not to dwell upon her two nights of freedom, sitting under the stars, warm and happy, when the whole world was full of possibility, and she had only to reach out and touch it. A knock at her door heralds the arrival of her mother, who, since she has returned, has taken to drooping and beginning every sentence with the same mournful plaint.

"Oh, Harriet," Charlotte Harbinger says, on a sigh. "Here you are. I still cannot understand why you wanted to run away."

Privately, Harriet cannot understand why she would want to remain. She has just witnessed what was almost a fistfight between her father and her uncle. It is the sort of behaviour that, if replicated by her or her brother, would get them both a beating and exile to their respective rooms for days.

"I missed the parrot, I told you," she says, between clenched teeth.

"Oh, Harriet," her mother repeats despairingly. "What will become of you?"

Harriet does not answer. The nights she spent being a ghost made her realise that her future was just waiting for her, out beyond the horizon. Everything seemed possible. Now, the high prison walls have closed in again.

"Your father says you are to put on your best dress and brush your hair. He is taking you and Hanover to call on great aunt this afternoon. You will apologise for your behaviour. You will beg her forgiveness. It is very important that you create a good impression, Harriet. Important to father. You must promise me that you won't speak out of turn or say any of your strange fanciful things. Do you promise, dear?"

Harriet stares into her mother's sad, watery eyes. *I am never getting married*, she thinks. "I will try, mother," she mutters.

"That's my good girl. And when you return, everything will be back to normal again and we will be the same happy little family that we were before, won't we?"

Harriet decides not to dignify this with a response. Her mother, interpreting her silence as agreement, smiles waveringly and retreats. Harriet goes over to the window and looks down. The dog, still chained to its kennel in the empty yard, lifts its head to the heavens and lets out a long, keening howl of despair. She knows exactly how it feels.

****

Euphemia Harbinger is fading. The bright flower that once bloomed so radiantly that it brought many men into eager submission, is dropping its petals, one by one. The hot fetid summer has exhausted her. Every new day seems to bring on some bodily indignity. She leaks, she creaks, she struggles to locate the words she needs to make her demands known, she can barely find the energy to lift her spoon to her lips, and when she does, everything tastes like pap.

She wakes in the night, listening for the footsteps of Death. Some days, she longs for him to snatch her up. And yet, even in the midst of decay, she is still not without power. Of a sort. Once, it was her beauty and gaiety that held men in sway. Now, it is her wealth. Once, people flocked to her door to be part of her life. Now, they come to see if she is dead.

Here is such a one. Arthur Harbinger, hotfoot from his confrontation with his younger brother, has managed to gain audience. He sits in her hot, stuffy bedroom, in the uncomfortable cane-bottomed chair (she has chosen it deliberately), his shoulders tense, his bony hands locked together between his knees. Wrapped in her soft cashmere shawls, and propped up on three feather pillows, she watches him, silently. A female deity, granting audience to a supplicant.

"Dearest aunt," the supplicant says, "I am delighted to see you looking so well and rested."

She deconstructs the now-familiar greeting. "But I expect you'd be far more delighted if I was laid out in my shroud, eh, Arthur? Both you and your brother."

He affects shock. "I am upset that you could possibly think this, dearest aunt, let alone say it."

"Oh, we who are dying are allowed the liberty of finally speaking our mind, don't you think? After all, what is there left for us to do? You have come to find out how your sister and I got on, is that not the truth? Come, do not dissemble. I am not so far gone that I can't smell a lie when it is thrust under my nose. Even when it is disguised as a bouquet."

Arthur Harbinger winces. He has brought a very expensive bouquet of hothouse flowers, purchased in haste on his way over. It lies on the chest of drawers.

"Your sister and I spent a very constructive and pleasant time together," the old woman says, slyly. "We reminisced about the past ~ old people like to reminisce and there was much I wanted to talk about with her. White kittens, coal holes, a dolls house that went up in flames, books she loved that were ripped up. It seems Wilhelmina had a very event-filled childhood. Do you not agree?"

"I think you should take whatever my sister may have imparted with a grain of salt, dear aunt," Arthur says, selecting from among the voices screaming in his head the tone of a reasonable man. "She was never a truthful child, so much of what she might have told you probably took place in her mind."

"But not all," the old woman counters, shooting him a shrewd searching glance. "Certainly not all. You did not carry out the final wishes of your father, which were to share things equally between the three of you, did you? As a result, your sister tells me that she has had to go out into the world and work hard to support herself."

Arthur Harbinger folds his hands. His face assumes an expression of such saintly virtuosity that it could have modelled for a stained-glass window. "I begged Sherborne not to do it, dear aunt. I said we should always endeavour to look after each other, but he was adamant. Wilhelmina had removed herself from the family home after an unfortunate disagreement with him. We did not know where she had gone. She went quite suddenly, in the night, without leaving an address. So, in her absence, we made the only decision we could."

"I see. Did you? But now, she has reappeared. So, what are you going to do to make amends?"

"If you care to give me her address," Arthur says, cunningly, "I shall see what can be done."

The old women snorts, in a very unladylike fashion. "I think not. You are more likely to lose it again, eh? Do not worry, I have already taken it upon myself to do what is right. It is clear, from speaking to your sister, that neither you nor your brother can be trusted."

The diamonds, Arthur thinks. *The beautiful, priceless diamonds, that could've been sold for a small fortune and then reinvested in some profitable business.* So, the girl told the truth: Wilhelmina has got her greedy undeserving claws upon the diamonds; they have gone.

"I am sorry to hear you say this, dear aunt," he says, making an effort to sound regretful while resisting the urge to place both hands round the wrinkled throat and squeeze the life out of her. "I assure you both I and my brother have nothing but your best welfare at heart."

"Really, Arthur? Is that why you have only now shown up at my door after all these years of living in the same city? When you smell my death approaching? I may be an old woman, near the end of my days, but I am not a complete imbecile. Now, be off with you. I want a rest, before your brother and his offspring turn up to ingratiate themselves, as I am sure they will."

Arthur Harbinger's smile is as false as that on a waxwork dummy. He rises, makes a small stiff bow, and walks to the door.

"And tell Rose to bring up my tea," the figure in the bed calls after him.

He clenches his jaw tight and descends the stairs. There is no sight of the housekeeper in the hallway. He finds her in the sitting-room, rearranging the china ornaments on the mantelpiece and exchanging words with the parrot. He relays the message. She instantly stops dusting and heads for the kitchen to make the tea. She does not show him out. A deliberate snub.

Arthur Harbinger collects his hat and stick from the hallstand and opens the front door. He contemplates slamming it, then has second thoughts. An idea suddenly strikes him. Somewhere, in the pile of paperwork on his desk, is the letter his aunt asked him to post some time ago, the one containing her signature. It is time to draw up another life insurance policy in her name. For an even larger premium, this time. He may have missed out on the diamonds, but one way or another, Arthur is going to profit from her demise. And sooner, rather than later.

****

Profiting from the demise of others is exactly what Lucy Landseer is investigating, in her first case as a consulting detective. She has ascertained, by judicious inquiries, that her client's stepfather has made multiple marriages. Two of his former wives have died ~ she cannot be certain that the circumstances were suspicious, although they were certainly auspicious as far as Mr Brooke was concerned.

As a result of being left a widower, he inherited a house in Hitchin, a bakery business, and another house in London. Not bad. Not bad at all, for a man who has done nothing to earn these things. Then, there is the wife still living. From her, he has also had a large sum of money. The question uppermost in Lucy's agile brain is this: what are Mr Brooke's plans for the future, once he has sold the current house and banked the money.

She is about to find out.

For the past two days, Lucy has been discreetly following Mr Francis Brooke. She now knows where he works ~ a rather drab office building off Tottenham Court Road that is let out to multiple businesses. She knows where he lunches ~ a rather run-down public house off one of the back courts. Today, however, Mr Brooke has chosen to desert the office for some retail therapy. She is on his trail.

Lucy has tracked him along Oxford Street, pausing as he entered one of the big department stores. She has then gone into the store and lurked behind pillars, hovered by merchandise, and affected great interest in stationery. Currently, her quarry is in the gentlemen's department, looking at cravats. Brooke has a way of insinuating himself round the displays of men's apparel as if he were about to spring on something.

It is now midday, and just as Lucy is wondering how long Mr Brooke is going to spend fingering ties and admiring his reflection, a fair haired, wearily-pretty, middle-aged woman, daintily dressed in a primrose silk dress, with a paisley shawl and light straw bonnet, cautiously enters the department. She walks with a stick and glances all around, as if seeking assistance. At once, Brooke is at her side. A look passes between them. Intrigued, Lucy edges nearer, positioning herself at the end of the counter and pretending to pore over a pile of men's linen handkerchiefs. She overhears Brooke saying,

"Amelia, my dearest girl ~ I thought I asked you to wait downstairs."

The woman replies faintly, "It is such a hot day, dear Francis, and you know I cannot stand for long. Besides, my head feels as if it is going to burst. I had to come in, if only to sit a while. Are we going to partake of luncheon soon? I am so hungry."

Francis Brooke pulls at his shiny brown moustache (Lucy is sure it is dyed). "Why don't you go up to the restaurant, dear girl. I shall just pay for these cravats and join you shortly."

Lucy follows Amelia-my-dearest-girl at a discreet distance, lowering her gaze as she enters the restaurant, where a pianist is entertaining the customers with a selection of sentimental tunes. She waits for the woman to be seated, then selects a single table close by. She orders a pot of tea and the cheapest sandwiches on the menu, (she may be permitted a certain amount of expenses in the course of her work, but she is not the sort of individual to exploit her clients).

In a short while, the woman is joined by Brooke, carrying a parcel. He lifts her gloved hand, and kisses it, letting his lips linger a little too long for Lucy to believe she is a family member. Then he slides into the opposite seat and clicks his fingers to summon the waitress. Lucy's top lip curls. She has always considered this to be a rather common gesture.

While the couple await the arrival of their food, Francis Brooke holds the woman's hand in his, peering adoringly up into her face. The lady modestly turns her cheek, upon which Lucy discerns a faint rose blush. He speaks to her in a low voice, which is extremely annoying for the eavesdropper at the next table, but by leaning in as far as she can without tipping over her chair, Lucy catches the words: *'selling the old house ... start our new life together ... waited so long.'*

The luncheon arrives. Brooke tucks in heartily, chatting around and sometimes during mouthfuls. His companion says very little, merely regarding him enraptured, while conveying very small squares of bread and butter into her mouth. The words 'besotted' come to mind. Also, the word 'fool', but Lucy reminds herself that this woman does not know what she knows, therefore the rather florid charms of Mr Brooke must seem to her to be completely genuine. Given her frail health, as evinced by the walking stick, and the minute amount she is eating, despite saying earlier that she was hungry, Lucy suspects that Mr Brooke has made, once again, a careful and deliberate choice of a future partner in life.

Eventually, the luncheon is finished. Mr Brooke rises, indicating that he will pay the bill and then go to the gentlemen's rest room. Lucy thinks fast. Somehow, she has to find out where this Amelia lives. An idea strikes her. She picks up an uneaten slice of buttered bread from her plate, lowers her veil, pulls her bonnet down, and rises, as if she is leaving. But as she passes the table, she drops her bread, butter side down, into the fair one's lap. She flinches. Lucy gasps, bringing both hands to her face.

"Oh no! Oh no! I apologise. What a terrible thing. Please forgive me." She leans over and attempts to retrieve the bread but somehow manages to spread the greasy butter even further. "Oh, I am so clumsy today!" She fishes in her bag. "Your lovely dress! Let me pay for the cleaning ~ oh, wait, I have no cards. Oh, what a silly girl I am. Perhaps you can give me your card and I will, I promise, recompense you."

The fair one purses her lips. "It really doesn't matter, Miss ..."

"But it does matter. It matters a great deal. May I trouble you for your card? I would never forgive myself if I did not make good the damage I have caused by my clumsiness."

The woman shrugs, but hands Lucy a small gold-rimmed visiting card. "It is really no matter, I assure you, but if you insist ..."

"Oh, I do, I do," Lucy assures her earnestly. "Thank you. You will be hearing from me, I promise you. An apology, if nothing else. Oh, I hope I have not spoiled the rest of your day."

Spotting Mr Brooke returning in the distance, she stuffs the card into her bag, pays for her food, and hastens back down the stairs to street level. So, it is as she suspected: Mr Brooke is already lining up his next victim. But he has reckoned without the force of nature that is Lucy Landseer. Hubris is finally going to meet its Nemesis. Yes indeed.

****

Meanwhile, over in Chelsea, Sherborne Harbinger stands outside the front door of his aunt's house. He is flanked on either side by the twins Hanover and Harriet, who have been drilled into submission by their stern papa. There is to be no wayward commenting this time, no straying from the practiced discourse. They wait to be let in. The sun shines. Sherborne sweats under his formal suit jacket, the macassar oil on his hair glistens wetly like snail slime. The twins fidget and glare at each other.

Minutes pass. Eventually, the door is opened by Rose, the housekeeper. Her face takes on a fixed expression. "My mistress is not receiving this afternoon," she announces.

But Sherborne, a man with pound signs imprinted on his retinal grain, is not going to be put off by a mere member of the servant class.

"We shall not disturb my aunt for long. My daughter has something she wishes to say. Please announce us."

Sherborne gives Harriet a sharp push in the back which sends her almost sprawling over the threshold and into the house. The housekeeper clamps her mouth together and goes upstairs. In a few minutes, she returns. "My mistress says only the little girl may go up. You must wait in the sitting room." The word 'reluctantly' hovers in the air looking for somewhere to land.

Harriet follows the rigid black-clad servant up the familiar stairs. Rose opens the bedroom door. "Miss Harriet Harbinger to see you, madam," she says primly. "I shall go and make your beef tea."

Even to Harriet's untrained eye, the old woman in the bed does not look well. Her cheeks seem to have sunken into her face. Her skin is yellowy-white, her eyes stare at the far wall, pale and expressionless. Yet, as soon as she sees Harriet, she appears to brighten. She hauls herself higher up in bed and pats the coverlet.

"Come and sit here, child. Let me look at you."

Harriet crosses the room and perches cautiously on the silken coverlet. She might look a bit scary, but at least the old woman doesn't appear to have anything visible to beat her with.

"I am sorry for the trouble I caused," Harriet says mechanically.

"Are you? What trouble was that? Remind me."

Harriet stares into the wrinkled face and sees a glimmer of something steely in the filmy eyes peering up at her.

"I broke into your house. I stole your food."

"So I gather! Rose said it was rats, but I knew better. Rats don't pour themselves glasses of milk. Nor do they take books from the shelves. What I do not understand is why you came here in the first place. Did you not think your family would be worried?"

Harriet scrunches up her face. "I just thought it would be nice to be somewhere else. Where I didn't keep getting into trouble. And I wanted to see the parrot."

"I see. You left a couple of books behind you."

"They are your books, not mine. I don't steal," Harriet says stoutly.

"You like reading?"

"I love it."

"I presume you have a lot of books at home?"

Harriet shakes her head. "Father has some in his study, and Hanover has a whole shelf of schoolbooks. I have a few books, but I have read them. They are mainly about Christian children. I am not allowed to borrow Hanover's books because he is studying to go to a good school and then to university. And father's books are about business and not suitable for a girl's mind, he says."

"I am sorry to hear it. A life without books is a life only half-lived," the old woman says softly, almost as if she is speaking to herself.

The room falls silent. Harriet plays with the corner of the counterpane.

"I have something for you," Great Aunt Euphemia continues. "Go and look on the chest of drawers over by the window."

Harriet goes. Her eyes light up when she sees the atlas. "For me?"

"For you. Rose discovered the books when she found your hiding place. I have no need of an atlas now, so I am giving it to you. One day, all the books in the house will be yours as well ~ but don't tell anybody. Let it be between the two of us. What do you say?"

Harriet picks up the precious book and hugs it to her starched pinafore'd chest. Her eyes are shining. Her heart is too full to speak. Gratitude fills her up, blossoms inside her. She turns her radiant face to the figure on the bed, who smiles, placing a thin, clawed finger to her lips.

"I like secrets. And I have kept enough of them in my life. I still do. Now, young Harriet, I think we have said all we need to say, and I hear Rose coming upstairs with my beef tea. It has been a pleasure getting to know you. I expect you will be returning home soon. As will I."

Harriet looks perplexed. "But ... isn't this your home?"

The old woman's mouth moves. "A different home, I mean."

Harriet thinks about this for a bit, but still doesn't understand. "When you go there, you will take the parrot with you? You won't let it die?"

"I promise the parrot won't die."

The housekeeper enters the room with a tray.

"Harriet is just leaving," her mistress says. "It has been a most pleasurable visit. Good-bye young lady. I hope you manage to find your pirate ship one day and sail it away to those far-off lands you spoke about."

To her surprise, because although she has been told frequently by her father to do it, she has always steadfastly refused to comply, Harriet bobs a curtsey. Then she walks quickly out of the room, carrying her book under her arm. It has not been made explicit, but she senses that this might be the last time she will ever see her great aunt, which also means that she will never again sleep in the small attic room, nor sit on the back step with her supper, perfectly content in her own company, staring up into the night sky. For a moment, the knowledge hurts so badly that she can't breathe. Despair rises up inside her, but she pushes it fiercely away.

Harriet enters the sitting room, where her father is standing by the empty grate contemplating something or other. Hanover is pushing his finger through the bars of the parrot's cage and pulling them back before the bird can peck them.

Sherborne Harbinger turns round and glares at her. "So, Harriet. You are back. I hope you have apologised to your great aunt for your excessively bad behaviour."

"I have apologised," Harriet repeats mechanically.

"And what, pray, have you got under your arm? A book? Have you stolen it? I cannot believe, after all you have put us through, that you have further blackened your character! Harriet ~ is there no end to your wickedness?"

"It was a present," Harriet protests.

"I very much doubt that. Indeed, I do. Hand it to me at once. I shall return it to great aunt."

Sherborne wrestles the book from his daughter. He opens it. Harriet can see something written on the flyleaf. He reads what is written, and his expression changes. He hands the atlas back to her without saying anything further. They push their way through the hurrying, unsmiling crowds, down the tired dusty streets until they arrive at the Excelsior Hotel, where Sherborne orders the twins to go to their rooms and prepare for dinner.

As soon as she reaches the sanctuary of her room, Harriet tips the atlas open at the first page, where she reads: *'A present to dear Harriet from her great aunt, Euphemia Harbinger. The whole world lies before you. Trim your sails and set your sights on the far horizon.'*

Later, when the hotel is quiet, and only the stars and moon are awake, Harriet sits on her bed, turning the pages of her atlas. It shows her where she has come from, but it tells her where she is going. She studies map after map. Then she opens her notebook and begins to write. She writes until she is too tired to write any more. Finally, she puts her head down on the pillow and sleeps.

****

Sleep, however, is the last thing on Lucy Landseer's mind. Her busy brain is bursting with ideas. Here she is sitting at her little desk in the corner of the living room. Supper has been consumed, and the dirty dishes lie on the draining board, awaiting someone's attention. Her Cambridge professor is stretched out on the rug, critiquing a manuscript. Every now and then, he utters a sigh and makes a note in the margin. It is hard work being professorial.

Meanwhile, Lucy is composing her latest article for *The Lady's Home Companion* magazine. She has been commissioned to write a monthly series of articles under the generic title: *The Lady visits …* Each one features a different London location. So far, the Lady has visited the British Museum (three times), Madame Tussaud's

Waxworks Exhibition, the Burlington Arcade and Regent's Park.

Now, the Lady is visiting Kensington Gardens, because it is summer and therefore the fashionable champêtre concerts, played by the band of the Household Cavalry, are taking place every Tuesday and Friday between 5 and 6pm. It is a good excuse to let her imagination linger on bright scarlet jackets, luxuriant moustaches, bonny brass buttons and shiny instruments. Lucy may have her own beau, nevertheless, there is something about a soldier ~ well, you know what soldiers are. She also knows what her readers like. They will like this article.

Time passes in companionable silence, apart from the odd expostulation from the professor. Eventually Lucy sets down her pen and looks round. "There. I have done," she says. "And now I must write to my first client. The case is proving to be even more intriguing than I first thought."

The professor smiles at her. "But you will not tell me what it is about?"

Lucy tosses her head coquettishly. "Oh no, I cannot do that. It is like a doctor/patient relationship: confidentiality must be observed at all times. But I believe we are in the endgame and once we have proceeded beyond that, well, perhaps I might share some details with you. Especially as you have provided me with the necessary information to fix Mr Brooke ~ I think I can tell you his name. How useful you are!"

"Your thanks must go to my colleagues in the Law Faculty."

"Then I do thank them, most heartily. It is always interesting to learn new facts. And now, if you have finished groaning over your manuscript, perhaps you might turn your attention to the pots in the sink? I shall join you just as soon as I have written my letter."

Lucy selects a piece of her special headed notepaper. She takes a fresh pen and, after chewing the end for a couple of seconds, begins to write. As she does so, her thoughts run upon the fates of the four unfortunate women whose lives have become entangled with Mr Francis Brooke. She has read (and indeed written) about faithless dishonourable men. Now she has encountered a real live one and finds him to be far nastier in fact than fiction.

Once she has finished her letter and sealed the envelope, she goes over to the window and leans out, taking a deep breath of warm night air. The window is latched open. The sounds of a city settling into itself filter into the room. *Out there are millions of people*, she thinks. *Some happy, some desolate.* She hears a bird carolling its evening song to the world. In the tiny pantry, the professor is clattering the pots and humming happily to himself. Lucy draws down the blind. *There is nothing I would change about my life*, she thinks. *Nothing at all. Not even if I could.*

****

Parliament is rapidly heading towards its summer recession. This means that everything slows down, everything feels looser at the seams. There are more jokes in the House, more bonhomie and back-slapping, longer times spent in the tea-rooms, less antagonism and name-calling. Everyone has their sights set on the break. Trips to Europe are discussed, renovations to country piles put forward, lists of house guests are exchanged. The odd book project is floated. Minds are focused on leisure and relaxation.

The Honourable Thomas Langland's mind is focused on Spartacus and his plans for the horse's future. This morning he is off to Knightsbridge, where he is meeting some like-minded friends at Tattersalls to view the horses for sale and discuss equine matters, leaving the business of his parliamentary office in the hands of his clerk (whose name he has still not bothered to remember).

Thus, the Replacement finds himself unexpectedly sitting behind the big mahogany desk, working his way steadily through two piles of papers, consisting of Hansard reports and letters from constituents. He has been charged with annotating the first pile, producing a summary of every debate, and dispatching a suitably concerned missive expressing sympathy in response to the second pile ~ which he is instructed to sign in the name of the MP, who hasn't and doesn't intend to, read them.

Time passes. The Replacement feels his concentration flagging. There is only so much insincerity you can fake before it becomes tedious, and your wrist starts to ache. He decides to get up and take a turn about the room. Whilst turning, he notices that one of the portraits is hanging slightly askew. He goes over, intending to straighten it. He has the sort of obsessive mind that can never bear to be in a room with crooked pictures, chairs not set straight to a table, and cutlery at an angle. In moving the picture to the left, he feels the edge of the frame scrape against something. Intrigued, the Replacement shifts it carefully back again, and sees a small wall-safe. The door has been left slightly open in a 'looser at the seams' way.

The Replacement goes into the outer office and returns with his high stool. He climbs onto it, reaches into the safe and removes a pile of letters, which he places on the Honourable Thomas Langland's desk. He sits back down, picks up his quill, because he does not feel secure without something to hold in his hand, and begins slowly and carefully to peruse the correspondence, setting aside one letter, then the next. As the pile diminishes, the frown between his brows deepens as the realisation dawns on him exactly what he is looking at. He had thought the answer to his friend's disappearance lay in the locked drawer in the mahogany desk. He now realises how wrong he was.

Here are letters from builders and developers asking Langland to use his influence as an MP to get them planning permission for various works. The letters offer rewards, some of them financial. Other letters convey the deep gratitude of the sender, clearly indicating that Langland has acceded to their requests. Some letters are from other MPs, expressing thanks to their esteemed colleague for putting them in the way of a nice house, or an opportunity to acquire a property at cost price for a family member.

One very poignant letter comes from a constituent, pleading with him not to sell the farm and the land that has been in his family for centuries. It is ill-spelt and on poor-quality notepaper, but desperation leaks from every line. The Replacement cross-references it to a letter from a developer, thanking Langland for arranging the sale of the farm and land and promising to give him first refusal on one of the fine brand-new houses to be built. The developer's name is Wm. Boxworth ~ a name that is familiar to him, though he cannot quite place it.

The Replacement racks his brains. Where has he seen that name before? Then he recalls where: on the hoarding surrounding the building site where his friend's body was discovered. He riffles through the rest of the correspondence and finds two more communications. Both are copies of confirmatory receipts of large sums paid by certain MPs to Mr Wm. Boxworth in return for shares in various developments in London and other major cities.

He is initially puzzled why Langland should have made copies of these receipts, which do not refer to him specifically by name, but after thinking about it for a while, he realises the copies are Langland's security. If, at any future time, an attempt is made to discredit him in the House, or elsewhere, he has only to hint at the existence of these copied letters, and he has a ready-made cohort of terrified MPs who will do all in their power to brush scandal away from his door because if they don't, it will also wash up at their door and ruin them as well. It is cunning and clever and shows a degree of ruthless connivance that goes way beyond his comprehension.

So finally, he understands what his friend was hinting at. The scale of corruption and cronyism is laid bare before his eyes. Langland is awarding lucrative building contracts in return for financial reward. He is also using his influence to act as an introductory bridge between certain opportunistic MPs and unscrupulous developers. Again, in return for money or favours. This is what his friend must've discovered. And somehow, Langland found out that he had discovered it. And that is why he died, because Langland's reputation and career are things he would wish to preserve at all costs. Even, it appears, at the cost of another man's life ~ but a man who was only a parliamentary clerk, so not of any value in the great scheme of things.

The Replacement suddenly feels cold, overwhelmed by the immensity of what he has discovered and the implications. His hands start shaking. The quill falls from his fingers, stuttering black ink over the pile of correspondence. Frantically, he grabs the blotter and tries to mop up the mess, but to no avail. The evidence cannot be erased. The moment Langland looks into the safe and sees the ink-stained letters, he will know that somebody has perused them, and it will be a matter of seconds to work out who.

Now he is in the same position as his friend. His life stands in the balance. A deep pit has opened at his feet, and he is teetering on its edge. He shuffles the letters together into a pile and replaces them in the wall-safe, making sure, as sure as he can, that they are in exactly the same order, and the safe is open at the exact angle he found it to be originally.

The Replacement takes his clerk's stool back into the outer office. He moves with difficulty, as if he is under water. He is in shock. When he finally goes back to Langland's desk, he sits hunched forward, trying to fit everything together. There is a tightness in his chest. A sense of vertigo. The words he is supposed to be writing dance in front of his eyes.

Finally, he can stand it no longer. He rises and rushes out, hatless, into the street, the air closing around him. The streets are thick with people. They loom at him, and then fall away. He feels as if he has something growing inside, waiting to be hatched. Reaching a deserted back-alley, he leans over and vomits next to the wall.

****

A few hours later, still on the same sunny summer afternoon, we find Miss Lucy Landseer, author and private detective, accompanied by Miss Rosalind Whitely, spinster and client. They are on their way to pay a morning call upon a third lady. They are wearing their finest clothes (in the case of Rosalind, her finest mourning clothes), because it will be important, if judged by first appearances, as many frequently do, that they appear credible.

The cab drops them on the outskirts of Belsize Park. Lucy consults her map and a small visiting card, then directs them up Haverstock Hill. They turn left by a small stationery and tobacconist shop and enter a pleasant road with houses set back from the pavement. The road is planted with trees. They stop outside Number 12.

"Well, here we are. You know what you have to do?" Lucy asks.

"Oh yes," Rosalind nods. Her mouth forms a determined line. She clutches her bag a little more firmly.

They open the gate, mount the four steps. Then, taking a deep breath, Lucy Landseer rings the doorbell.

The door is opened by a small maid of all work, who gazes wonderingly at the two smartly clad young women. Lucy favours her with her most charming smile, the one that gets her admitted to so many places where she should not, by rights, have entered.

"We have come to see your mistress. Here is my card. I believe she is expecting us. Please announce us, if you'd be so kind."

The maid trots off, carrying the card cautiously. They step into the hallway. Lucy mentally makes a note of the dark green wallpaper, the small table with its silver filagree basket for visiting cards, the green and black patterned floor tiles and elaborate overmantel with gold framed mirror. Everything is slightly old-fashioned, but of good quality.

The maid returns. The two visitors are shown into a drawing-room, where they find Miss Amelia Ferry, her walking cane at her feet, sitting in a dark red upholstered chair, an open book on her lap. A tapestried fire screen and an embroidered runner along the dark marble mantelpiece bear witness to her sewing skills. There is a piano, a lacquered desk, and several sofas. The window is heavily draped with muslin, giving the room a shaded atmosphere.

As they enter, a small brown and white terrier gets up from its spot on the hearthrug, stretches its back legs, then trots over to make their acquaintance. Lucy immediately squats down and fondles its soft ears. She is very fond of dogs. Real and fictitious. The dog licks her hand enthusiastically. It is watched from a distance by the invalid.

"Oh, what a *lovely* little dog," Lucy smiles, glancing up from her position on the floor. "What is her name?"

"Jess. She is my constant companion. I do not enjoy the best of health and am obliged to spend long periods resting. My little dog makes such times more endurable. Miss Landseer and Miss Whitely, please sit down. I confess to being a little at a loss as to why you are paying me a call. I do not recollect meeting either of you before. Do you belong to some local Church charitable committee? Have you come to appeal for a donation?"

"No, we are not from any such organisation," Rosalind says.

"But we have come to appeal to you," Lucy adds. "Let me explain. We believe you are acquainted with a certain gentleman called Mr Francis Brooke?"

The invalid's cheeks colour up. "Yes, I know him. Why do you ask?"

Lucy gives Rosalind Whitely a meaningful go-on-tell-her glance. Rosalind digs in her bag and proffers a photograph. "Perhaps you recognise Mr Brooke? He is my stepfather. The lady with him was his wife ~ my mother. She is dead now."

"I noticed that you were in mourning, Miss Whitely. I am so sorry. To lose a parent is a tragic event. I lost both of my dear parents to cholera when I was very young. They were missionaries in India." The invalid stares down at the photograph, a puzzled frown gathering between her brows. "When did you lose your mother, Miss Whitely?"

180

"Six months ago," Rosalind says.

"But ... Mr Brooke wears no mourning band. He has never mentioned a stepdaughter. And I am sure he told me that his wife died several years ago. I do not understand."

"Different wife," Lucy says. "He probably meant this one," and she hands over the photograph taken by the church lych-gate. "This lady was Mr Brooke's second wife. My client's mother was his third wife."

"Your 'client'?" the invalid queries.

"I am a consulting private detective, Miss Ferry," Lucy says. "Miss Whitely, whom you see here before you, engaged me to discover whether her mother died in suspicious circumstances."

The invalid's face flushes. "I am sure nothing of that sort could ever be suspected of Fran ~ Mr Brooke! You must be mistaken, young woman. I may not have known him for long, but I am a very good judge of character, and I am quite sure he is an honourable man."

"Is he?" Lucy says, her eyes widening. "I wonder whether his *first* wife, who is still alive by the way, and who has shown me her marriage certificate to prove her marital status, would agree with that?"

The invalid's mouth quivers. "I ... I ... what are you telling me?"

"That I believe, Miss Ferry, you have been the innocent and hapless victim of a ruthless and callous seducer," Lucy says, (the words come straight out of her novel). "My investigation of Mr Brooke has revealed a similar pattern of behaviour: he befriends a woman who is in a position like yourself: single, with no immediate family, but in possession of independent means or property. If she is in poor health, so much the better. He marries her, and then, upon her death, he takes control of everything she owns. So far, he has enriched himself at the expense of three women. We, his step-daughter and I, are here to make sure he doesn't do the same to you."

"Indeed, Miss Landseer only speaks the truth. Mr Brooke now owns my family home, the house where I was born and grew up. The house I have lived in all my life, where my dear Mama passed away. And he is going to sell it and turn me out into the street," Rosalind says.

Lucy gives her an approving nod. So far, so sticking to the script.

"Except, of course, that he doesn't, and he can't," she adds. "Because he was never properly married to Miss Whitely's mother in the first place. I believe that Mr Brooke is planning to repeat his crime ~ for bigamy is a crime, Miss Ferry, make no mistake. If he intends to marry you, he does so in the full knowledge that he has a wife still living. That is why we have come to call upon you. We wish to save you from the clutches of this vile man and put an end to his unscrupulous behaviour towards innocent women, once and for all."

The invalid's face is now chalk white. Her hands clutch compulsively at her book. The little dog goes to sit at her feet, looking up into her face. It gives a small, anxious whine. Immediately, Lucy darts over to the small desk and pours some water from a carafe.

"Drink this, dear Miss Ferry. Regain your composure. Then let us tell you of our plan."

The invalid takes a sip of water. "I am recovered. I am listening."

"It is my step-father's birthday this Saturday," Rosalind says. "Although I expect you know this."

Amelia Ferry sighs. "I do indeed. He has told me, and I was intending to go into the West End after your visit to purchase a present."

"I would not bother, if I were you. Miss Ferry," Lucy says drily. "But you might like to come to the tea-party my client is arranging. It will be in the garden of her house, and I believe it will be a memorable occasion. One that will linger long in the mind of the birthday celebrant. Yes, indeed. Please say you will attend?"

The invalid looks despairingly from Lucy to Rosalind. "I hope you understand that I am finding all this very hard to believe, ladies. You enter my house, complete strangers, unknown to me, and tell me such dreadful stories! How do I know you are telling me the truth? It sounds so unlikely that Mr Brooke ~ the kind gentleman I have grown so fond of, could be guilty of all the terrible events you describe."

"Come to tea on Saturday," Lucy replies firmly. "For we hope to invite another guest also. One whose presence Mr Brooke will find it very hard to explain away. She will bring the proof that will convince you that every word we've uttered is the truth ~ the whole truth and absolutely the truth. Will you come?"

A short while later, having secured Amelia Ferry's agreement to attend the birthday tea, together with her promise not to communicate with Mr Brooke in any way until the day itself, Lucy and Rosalind take their leave.

"I hope she is a woman of her word," Rosalind Whitely says, as they head for the omnibus stop.

"I am sure she is," Lucy nods. "She will come, if for no other reason than to prove us wrong and exonerate him in her eyes. And now, I must write post-haste to the first Mrs Brooke and invite her to attend the party also."

"If she is the 'first' one," Rosalind says darkly. "Perhaps there are others we do not yet know about? Have you thought of that?"

Lucy has indeed thought about it. "Possibly there are, yes. But let us not be greedy, Miss Whitely," she says. "We have enough wives for our purpose."

****

While Miss Lucy Landseer and Miss Rosalind Whitely are on their mission of enlightenment, the Honourable Thomas Langland, MP is heading towards his office, prior to catching the early train back to the family mansion in the countryside. He has had a busy and productive day. A small syndicate has been set up and the money negotiated to purchase the mare he has set his heart upon.

He has visited his tailor and shirtmaker, spending the tail-end of the afternoon at his Club. Parliament is going into recess, finally, and he intends to spend the end of the summer at his country house with his horses. And occasionally his wife and children. Langland enters the building, mutters a cursory greeting to the colourless clerk who is scratching away at his desk, before entering his office, where a fresh pile of reports awaits his attention.

Uttering a sigh, he picks up the top one, his mouth curling in disdain as he sees it is a memorandum from the *Committee for Providing Small Orphan Children with Useful Employment*. He pats down his pockets to locate his cigar case, but upon opening it, finds it empty. Damn. He remembers giving his last cigar away to that rogue Boxworth. He goes to the door and summons the Replacement.

"Look … umm … just cut along to my tobacconist in the Strand and pick me up a box of my usual cigars," he says. "Tell him who it's for. And make it snappy, would you. Lot of paperwork to get through before I pack up here, and I don't want to miss my train."

The Replacement nods, without making any eye contact. He claps his hat onto his head and hurries out into the street. Reaching the shop, he enters and requests a box of Langland's usual cigars. To his surprise, however, the shopkeeper takes a step back and stares at him suspiciously, folding his arms as he does so.

"Now, wait a bit. Wait a bit, young sir. You ain't the MP, nor you ain't t'other young gent what comes in when he don't, now are you?"

The Replacement agrees that this is indeed the case.

"I ask coz the cigars in question are the most expensive and exclusive in the shop, and I can't just go handing them out to any Tom Dick or Harry who comes in SAYING they want them for their master, can I? After all, how do I know you are the genuine article?"

The Replacement applies his mind to the problem. After a few minutes' cogitation, he reaches into his pocket and hands a folded letter to the shopkeeper. "This is from Mr Langland, requesting a report from the Treasury to be supplied to him. I dealt with it this morning. You can see the heading on the notepaper, and his signature. I am unlikely to have this in my possession if I didn't work in his parliamentary office, don't you think?"

The shopkeeper studies the letter, glances again at the Replacement, then nods. He reaches up to one of the shelves behind the counter and lifts down a wooden box.

"Here you go, young man. Ten Cuaba cigars and you won't find anything finer in the whole of London." He pauses, then leans across the counter and beckons the Replacement to come close. "Funny you should come in for them. I had two Scotland Yard detectives in my shop a while back, asking about these very cigars."

The Replacement stares. "What did they want to know?" he asks, trying to keep his voice disinterested.

The shopkeeper leans his elbows on the counter and settles into his story. "Well, between you and me, I think they were investigating a murder. Not that they said so, far from it, but I could tell it was very serious. You work in a shop, you soon get to be a bit of an expert on people. They were hiding their real reason for coming in. Don't know how the cigars fitted in of course, but then I'm not

185

a detector, just a humble purveyor of fine tobacco and smokes."

"Yes, indeed," the Replacement murmurs, backing speedily out of the shop, the box in his hand. He sets off back to his place of work. Sometimes you become aware of a pattern forming around you, but you can't quite tell what it is. He recalls that a cigar was mentioned in the description the police officer gave him. At the time, he did not focus on it, being more concerned with the murder of his friend. Now, he takes his retentive and obsessive mind back to the actual words spoken on that occasion, as he hands the box of cigars to Langland, who as usual, barely looks up from his desk.

The Replacement returns to the outer office, selects a piece of paper, and writes in his neat, clerkish hand:

Dear Constable Williams

At our meeting a few days ago, you mentioned, I believe, the presence of a cigar, or part of the same at the site where the murder of my friend took place. I would be grateful if you could tell me some more details. Do you happen, by chance, to know the brand of cigar? I have a particular reason for asking this question, strange as it may seem. I express my gratitude in advance.

He signs the letter, blots it, and places it in a sealed envelope, which he addresses to Constable Tom Williams at Scotland Yard. The reply from the young constable, when it is eventually delivered, confirms his suspicions, although by the time that happens, Langland will have left London and be safely ensconced on his country estate with his horse and family.

After reading the letter, the Replacement thinks long and hard about the case being closed. So be it then. It is not in his timid nature to return to Scotland Yard and insist on it being reopened. Besides, he tells himself, he has no actual proof to offer, just a set of coincidences, which Langland would deny. It would be his word against a well-known and popular MP. The detectives would send him away. Then he would be dismissed from his employment and spend the rest of his life hiding in shadows while looking over his shoulder, waiting for the same fate to befall him as befell his friend. So, dispensing justice must now be up to him. He feels his life twisting down to this point, as he turns over various possibilities in his mind, and wonders how to go about it, and what, if anything, he has to lose.

****

The working day ends. Here are Detective Sergeant Jack Cully and Constable Tom Williams leaving Scotland Yard together. There is a reason for this, and it also has to do with closed cases and a sense of justice denied.

Cully is anxious that he might be losing Constable Tom Williams. After all the time and effort he has put into training and encouraging the young police officer, he fears the young man might be feeling disillusioned with his prospective choice of career. He has, indeed, mentioned that he is not sure he sees a future for himself in the detective division. So, one afternoon a few days previously, Cully had sought him out, and invited him for supper.

The invitation has been accepted with alacrity, and now master and pupil are threading their way through the stream of home-going clerks, crossing the river and entering a world where cobbles turn to asphalt and setted stone; a world of small but respectable houses with their whited steps, milk cans hung on the area railings and flowering geraniums in pots on windowsills.

They pass hoardings advertising exotic soaps and curry pastes, they see women with baskets of bread, men hurrying from the docks, or lounging in doorways with their heads bare, smoking clay pipes and watching the world pass them by. Everywhere new yellow brick houses are springing up, new shops opening, new cuttings traversed by planks where new railway lines are being excavated, new sewers being laid. Only the tall sky-stabbing steeples of old churches are left to mark the places where the former great city existed, now swiftly being swept away by its brash replacement.

"When I first came to London, all this used to be fields and market gardens," Jack Cully says. "Who knows what it will look like when my daughters are my age? Doubt I'd recognise it."

The men turn the corner of Cully's street, and stop at the small terraced house. There are two little girls sitting on the step, waiting. One has a stick of chalk and is instructing the other into the mysteries of writing her letters. They both spring up, regarding the tall policeman shyly from under their eyelashes.

"Vi, Primmy, this is Constable Tom Williams. He's coming to have his supper with us tonight," Cully says, ushering the young man through the gate and into the house, where their nostrils are assailed with the fragrant smell of baking.

Emily Cully emerges from the kitchen, wiping her hands on her apron. She greets them both, one with a kiss, one with a warm smile. "You are very welcome in our house, Mr Williams," she smiles. "Jack has often spoken about you. May I take your hat and coat? Now, girls, spit-spot, let's have those hands washed, then sit up to the table."

Over a tasty supper of boiled chicken and green peas, Emily gently teases his back story out of the young officer. She does it with such skill and subtlety that Jack Cully once again wonders why there isn't a female branch of the detective division. If there ever were one formed, his wife would definitely be chief inspector.

Cully is genuinely surprised to discover that the young officer comes from a good middle-class family living in Norwich (which explains his excellent written ability). That he wanted to be part of the police force from an early age and, as soon as he was old enough, bade farewell to his birthplace and set off for London to join Scotland Yard. Cully has worked with young Tom for weeks, but he never knew that before this evening.

Over a luscious gooseberry pie, Emily moves the conversation on, using her experience of being married to Jack Cully to talk about the disappointments and frustrations of her husband's work. She never mentions what Jack Cully has told her about the young man's state of mind, nor indicates that she has any purpose other than making polite conversation with a guest.

"In all the years we've been married, Jack has never had a murder that didn't follow him home at night," she says. "Sometimes, I wake to find him tossing and turning; sometimes, he takes himself out of the house ~ he calls it 'walking the case'. Mr Stride does it as well. Jack says the night air helps to clear his mind. Of course, it isn't easy, the work. I know that more than many. I met my husband while he was investigating the murder of my dearest friend. Many a time I feared that the killer wouldn't be found, but he was. In the end, he was."

The young man never takes his eyes of her face. "And if he hadn't been found? If your husband hadn't caught him? What then? How would you have felt?"

Emily cocks her head to one side. "Why then, sooner or later, he'd have had to face a higher court and a greater judgement than any on this earth. And the punishment would not be for a while, but for all of eternity."

She cuts him another generous piece of pie.

"I am so proud of my Jack. And I am so glad I became his wife. There is no greater profession than his, in my opinion. You are just starting out, but even so, every time you walk through those doors into Scotland Yard, I'm sure you must think of all the good men who have gone before you, faithfully tracking down criminals and making the city a better place for all of us. And I am equally sure some of them are watching you and cheering you on."

It is late when Jack Cully finally returns home from walking the young constable to the nearest omnibus stop. Emily is still up, finishing smocking the tiny dress. Cully pauses in the doorway, watching her bent head, seeing her nimble fingers plying the needle. Even after all the years of marriage, she still possesses the power to astonish him.

"That was just right, what you said, Em," he remarks. "It was exactly what young Tom needed to hear. I think your words have put new heart into him. You did a good thing tonight, and I thank you for it. And I believe so will he, one day."

Emily Cully smiles serenely up at him, and folds up her sewing, before gently suggesting that as he has returned, she will now go up to bed, and by the way, the dishes still need washing.

****

Meanwhile, what news of Micky Mokey, music hall artist and his room-mate Little Azella? For them, life in the hectic world of mass entertainment moves at its usual frenetic pace. Several performances every day, with the audiences morphing from families who join in enthusiastically with Micky Mokey's popular ditties and gasp at the aerial agility of Little Azella, to drunken youths who heckle and mock and make lewd suggestions as Little Azella flies through the air on her silver wires.

Afterwards, there is the long trudge back to their lodgings, keeping their heads down, saying little, both preoccupied with their own internal thoughts. They have taken to stopping briefly at the same late-night coffee stall, which stays open to serve the night-time crowd of brightly painted backstreet butterflies, who congregate there at the end of their working shift before slinking off to frowsy rooms in squalid alleys to sleep off the night's business until emerging into the sunshine again.

Mickey Mokey is customarily the recipient of much attention. His youthful demeanour, and delicate features generate a lot of amusement from the coffee drinkers, who regularly offer to take him round the corner and make a proper man of him. So far, he has managed not to succumb to their raucous blandishments.

The two performers drink their coffee and eat the thick slices of buttered bread supplied by the elderly woman and her husband manning the stall, before creeping quietly through the front door of the lodging-house and climbing the dark stairs that smell of all the cabbage and all the mutton and all the beef ever consumed within its walls, until eventually they reach the attic room and fall into their beds.

****

It is Thursday night. Songs have been sung, aerial ballets performed. The chairman has pounded his gavel on the wooden table and rung his bell for the final time. The music hall lights have been extinguished, the costumes hung up, stage makeup removed. Mickey Mokey and Little Azella set out on the familiar journey. Their contract is coming to an end, like the long hot summer. In a short while, the music hall will briefly close its doors while the sets and flats and costumes are got ready for the upcoming Christmas season. The two performers will have to find another venue.

They discuss the possibilities as they walk.

"I fink we should look outside London again," Little Azella says. "I was talking to one of the dancing girls ~ she says Liverpool is a fine place. Lots of halls and the lodgings is much cheaper." She shoots a sideways glance at her companion. "Oi, you listenin' to me?"

Mickey Mokey nods. "I'm listening."

"No, you ain't," Little Azella says, reaching up to nudge him in the ribs. "And I know why. When are you going to give it a rest?"

"When it is over," Mickey Mokey responds. "When I see him leaving the hotel with his luggage in his hand and his tail between his legs. When I know that he has failed to get what he came for. Then it will be over."

"But you may never know," Little Azella says craftily. "What then?"

Mickey Mokey shakes his head. "I shall know, Little Azella. Either I shall see it for myself, or I will find out some way or another ~ maybe I shall sense it, I don't know. But I can't be easy in my mind until it is done."

Little Azella pulls a face in the darkness. "Well, all wot I can say is it'd better be done soon. We only got a few more weeks, and then we're out of the theatre and out of a job."

Mickey Mokey turns to face her. "We will be alright, Little Azella. Haven't we always got work? Don't worry yourself. Trust in the stars."

Little Azella slips her hand into his and gives it a squeeze. "You and your bloomin' stars!" she scoffs.

They are just about to turn into the road leading to Mrs Brimmer's lodging-house when suddenly, a figure rushes at them out of the darkness. Mickey Mokey automatically steps in front of Little Azella, raising his fists in a defensive gesture. But the man is not interested in them nor in their meagre possessions. He doesn't even seem to be aware of their presence. He stares straight ahead and utters a low cry of anguish as he rushes by them.

Mickey Mokey stares into his face as he passes, and the expression in the man's eyes and the pallor of his complexion makes his blood run cold. He looks like a tenant with a short lease on life. It is like meeting something gruesome in a graveyard.

"Who the 'ell was that?" Little Azella asks, as they continue on their way.

"Dunno. But I wouldn't like to be thinking whatever he's thinking," Mickey Mokey says, shaking his head. The desperation in the man's face made him glad that his own life, however precarious, had not sunk to such depths.

All the way back to the lodging-house, the encounter plays in his mind on an ever-repeating loop. It is as if a man knocks your elbow in a crowded street and you catch only a glimpse of his face, but the memory of it stays with you like a bruise. There is always someone worse off than you, he reflects. Maybe tonight, he had seen that person.

Meanwhile, the Replacement (for it is he) slows to a walking pace. He is huddled into his coat. It is a light night, the gas-flares muttering in a breeze from the river. Since he has read the incriminating letters hidden away in Langland's secret safe, and since he has received the confirmatory communication from Constable Williams, he has taken to walking the streets at night, falling insensibly into the habit. He would rather do without sleep than wake screaming as he falls into some pit, his head gnawing at itself. He no longer trusts his night-time self. So he walks and walks, the city seeming to echo his fear.

Sometimes, he is sure he is being followed. He dives into dark alleyways, ears strained for footsteps, eyes searching for some dark figure. He listens. He hears the silence listening back. The nights are short and full of sounds. Occasionally, he walks while asleep on his feet ~ the only reason he can imagine for ending up in some strange location, where small houseless children, ghosted with moonlight, crouch round a broken sewer pipe, black with slime. He is an outcast, just like them. They stare at him, their eyes feral.

On other nights, he passes construction sites surrounded by wooden hoardings covered with posters. He drifts past dark doorways, sensing within them the presence of people like him, who did not intend to show their faces, but shied away from the light, retreating deeper into their world of shadows. He pulls his hat low over his brow, fearful of being recognised or worse still, pitied.

He goes down endless successions of sombre and deserted streets, sometimes crossing bridges with the murky river flowing sullenly underneath. He traverses wildernesses of bricks and mortar, occasionally hearing the heavy regular footfall of a policeman on night duty.

He walks through parks, trees overlapping the sky. He hears singing, the shouts of belated parties of revellers; sometimes he catches glimpses of passing faces caught by the light of a streetlamp or a shop window. He keeps his head down, passing from shadow to light and back into shadow again. His life has fallen away into itself. He thinks of his dear dead friend, of their shared conversations, their hopes and dreams. And always, he sees the smile fading in the shadow of his friend's face as the silence rises and rises behind him.

****

The Saturday of Mr Francis Brooke's birthday arrives finally, fine and clear, and while the celebrant is at work, preparations for the momentous tea-party are in hand. Rosalind Whitely has ordered food for the event to be supplied by a local baker and confectioner, for she is far too nervous to trust herself to be in charge of a breadknife.

The cake, a marvel of pink and white icing has been delivered the day before, and now sits on a larder shelf. His stepdaughter, under instruction from Lucy, has persuaded Brooke that a small celebration is all that she feels appropriate, given the recent demise of his wife, her mother. Faced with her request, Brooke has been forced to agree, though he has told her that he may well only be able to attend for a brief time as 'work commitments' will probably draw him from the house soon after.

By two o'clock, the scene is set. A table is laid in the garden and covered with the best cream lace tablecloth. The chairs and places are all ready. Crustless sandwiches, little cakes, tarts and gingerbread biscuits are plated up, and waiting under clean muslin cloths to keep off the insect population. Rosalind, in a dress of white muslin and a straw bonnet comes out of the small conservatory and casts a critical eye over the preparations. She is satisfied. All that remains is for the principal guest to appear.

At half-past two, the time he usually gets back from his Saturday half-day, Brooke strides up the path and turns the key in the front door, to be greeted by his stepdaughter, who suggests they adjourn to the garden, where tea is ready and waiting. Brooke discards his hat and summer jacket and follows her into the small sunlight garden.

"What is all this?" he says, gesturing at the table. "I thought you told me a small celebration was appropriate. Are we now expecting company?"

"Please sit down, stepfather," Rosalind says calmly. "All will be revealed shortly. Now, while we wait for the guests to arrive, pray tell me about your morning's work? I hope it was not too hot in your office."

Brooke frowns. "What are you going on about, Rosalind? I repeat ~ why are there all these places set?"

As if in reply, the conservatory door opens and Miss Amelia Ferry steps cautiously down into the garden. At the sight of her, Brooke rises, a look of alarm on his face.

"Amelia? What on earth are you doing here?"

Miss Ferry walks across the lawn, leaning heavily upon her stick. "It is your birthday, Francis. I am here to celebrate it with your stepdaughter. The one you never told me about."

She lowers herself into a wicker chair and stares up at him. "Just as you never told me about your wife, her mother. Who only died recently. Far too recently for any respectable gentleman to think of entering into a new relationship, let alone make promises to another woman, as you have done to me."

"What the devil is this?" Brooke exclaims, glaring furiously at Rosalind. "What damned lies have you been spreading about me?"

"Nothing but the truth, Mr Brooke," comes a clear voice from behind him.

Brooke whirls round as Lucy Landseer enters the garden. She nods a greeting to the two women.

"Who the hell are you?" he demands.

"This is Miss Lucy Landseer," Rosalind says sharply. "She is a private consulting detective, hired by me when I became suspicious of your conduct after my mother died. She has worked tirelessly on my behalf and is here as a guest in my house. I should appreciate it if you would lower your voice and treat her with respect."

Mentally applauding her client, Lucy pulls out another white basket chair and sits down.

Brooke's face is now the colour of the crimson peonies growing by the wall. "A detective? What the ...? *Your* house? What do you mean *your* house? It is MY house ~ and don't you forget it, young lady. I inherited this house when your mother passed away."

"Ah," Lucy interrupts, raising a cautionary finger. "There is some problem about that. You see, Mr Brooke, it appears that you might have been ~ how shall I put it, a little careless in respect to some previous marriages. For instance, here I have the photograph of one of your former wives ~ the one before you married Miss Whitely's mother. I am sure you recognise her?"

Brooke snatches up the photograph, glances at it, then tosses it aside. "So what? She died many years ago, leaving me free to marry again."

"But you are not free, Francis, are you?"

And exactly on cue, Mrs Leonora Brooke, in full feathers, frills and war-paint comes out of the house and strides into the garden. "Yes, well may you look afraid! You thought you'd seen the last of me after you deserted me and ran off with our savings. But here I am, thanks to Miss Landseer, who tracked me down. So, whatever your little games are, I am come to put an end to them, once and for all."

"Bigamy is a criminal offence, Mr Brooke," Lucy takes up the narrative. "It comes under the Offences Against the Person Act of 1861 and carries a sentence of seven years penal servitude." (Oh, the usefulness of a Cambridge professor with access to law lecturers!)

Francis Brooke stares from one female face to another but finds no hint of sympathy in any of them.

Eventually, he turns back to face Leonora Brooke. "You can't prove any of this! It's your word against mine!"

"Well, here is our marriage certificate to show we are still man and wife in the eyes of the law," Leonora Brooke says, fishing a document out of her reticule and waving it in his direction. "I am happy to show it to any judge in any court in the land. Now what do you have to say?"

"We are not interested in what he has to say," Rosalind breaks in. "Please pack what you need overnight, Mr Brooke, and then leave this house ~ *my* house, at once. The maid will relieve you of the front door key on your way out. I never want to see you here in the future. I am prepared to send the rest of your things on when you have a forwarding address. But that is all. Go now. And do not darken my door again!"

Brooke bares his teeth in a grimace. "You will regret this, Rosalind. By God, you will regret it! As for the rest of you ... you ... bunch of ..." words fail him. Brooke gives them all a venomous glare, then marches back into the house.

"Well done, ladies," Lucy says quietly, as the conservatory door bangs shut after him. "You have seen off a craven liar and a cheating rogue."

"It does seem a shame that he will be at liberty to repeat his behaviour, though," Rosalind remarks. "I wonder how many other poor women will be caught in his snares?"

"He won't be going far, don't you worry," Leonora Brooke says grimly. "I took the liberty of arriving with a couple of local constables. They are waiting in the street to apprehend him as soon as he leaves the house. I have laid charges with a magistrate, and I will see him in court, you see if I don't! He abandoned me, he robbed me, and he has made me suffer. Now I will turn the tables on him. Seven years, I think you said, Miss Landseer?"

"Well done, Mrs Brooke!" Lucy claps her hands. "Nicely played. I congratulate you. And you too, Miss Ferry ~ you have played your part to perfection as well; thank you both for coming here today."

"Oh, my heart, my heart ~ it beats so fast," Miss Ferry gasps, laying a trembling hand to her bosom.

"Then let me give you a refreshing cup of tea at once," Rosalind says, picking up the silver teapot. She fills four cups. Adds cream and sugar, and hands them round. "But before we tuck into this lovely spread, I wish to propose a toast. Ladies ~ I invite you to raise your teacups and join me in saluting Miss Lucy Landseer ~ the best private consulting detective in London!"

Blushing, Lucy bows her head modestly as the three women toast her success in best Indian tea. Then, cloths are removed, plates are passed round, and the celebratory feasting begins.

****

A Sunday morning. The Replacement has grown to hate Sundays. The city closes around him: shops, businesses, everything is shut and quiet. The streets are depopulated. London is like some ruined city, or a city under curfew ~ as if an old plague has risen from its earthy bed and come back to stalk mankind.

Time is measured in church bells. In women hurrying from cookhouses with covered basins. He eats his own meagre luncheon, purchased the night before and pores over his diary, in which he has written down various imaginary scenarios, all leading ultimately to the death of his employer, Thomas Langland MP. Most of them are composed in the white-hot fury of desperation in the small hours of the morning. In the cold light of day, none of them look viable.

The Replacement sits in his room, watching the light fade, searching for a way forward. His mind turns over possibilities and alternatives, sifting them like a panhandler, waiting for that one sudden glint of gold. He hears the rattle of a lone cab going by. Horses' hooves strike the cobbles. He listens intently, until the sound fades to nothing. He waits until the nothing is less than nothing. His face doesn't change, but something shifts inside him. He takes his coat and hat, places a couple of items from the table into his pockets. The Replacement crosses the room. Then he reaches for the handle of his door and goes out, closing the door behind him.

****

The August night is warm ~ not as warm as heretofore, but still warm enough for the upstairs window of Thomas Langland's first floor bedroom to be open. He lies on his bed, at the front of the house, sleeping peacefully. In her room at the back of the house, his wife sleeps. Next door, also at the back, the children and their governess sleep. In the attics overhead, the servants sleep.

Outside, a pale crescent moon shines down upon the carp pond, the sundial, the apple orchard, the maze, and the black-clad figure crossing the lawn. The figure makes its way round to the side of the house, where the racehorse is stabled. Arriving there, it stops and whistles softly. Inside the loose box, the bay stallion gets to his feet and wickers in response.

The figure quietly eases back the stable bolts and enters the loose box. A few seconds later, the stallion emerges, and trots off into the distance. The night wears on. Then someone sets up a cry just under Langland's window: "Fire! Fire! The stable is on fire! Help!" Thomas Langland wakes, grabs his dressing gown, and rushes from the house in blind panic, heading for the stable where his precious racehorse is housed.

He reaches the loose box. Smoke is billowing out. The door is open, but fearing the worst, Langland steps over the threshold, peering forward into the dark, smoke-filled stable and calling the horse's name. Someone steps silently up behind him and gives him a sharp push. Someone throws a lighted torch over his head, which lands on the bales of straw that have been piled up in the centre of the stable floor. Finally, someone closes the stable doors and slides the double bolt across.

Next day, the damage done in the night is revealed. The fire has destroyed the entire stable block, loose box, and tack room. Luckily, none of the carriage horses, or the children's riding ponies, which are all housed in a different part of the grounds, have been touched. The racehorse, who is at first assumed to have perished in the flames, is subsequently discovered a short distance away in a field, peacefully cropping the grass. Nobody has a clue how he got out of the blazing inferno that completely destroyed his stable. All that remains of his owner, alas, are some charred and blackened bones, from which it is assumed he perished trying to put out the flames.

The fire will, of course, be duly investigated by the local constabulary, but no conclusive evidence will ever be discovered as to what exactly occurred on that tragic night. It was known that Mr Langland sometimes liked to walk round the estate after dark, and enjoyed smoking a cigar before retiring, so it is assumed that a spark from a match, carelessly tossed, must have started the blaze that trapped him. The coroner will therefore conclude that the death of Thomas Langland, MP was the result of an extremely unfortunate accident.

Sadly, the unfortunate accident will result in wider repercussions. Also unfortunate. For some. For without its illustrious figurehead to promote it and give it the validity needed in a competitive business environment, the Boxland Joint Stock Railway Company will eventually hit the buffers, causing the failure of a private City bank, and flinging into ruin the major shareholders who invested all they had, or all they thought they might have, along with it.

****

But these things are yet to be. Let us resume our tale on a bright morning, shortly after the demise of Thomas Langland. Here is London's finest female detective, Miss Lucy Landseer, mounting the stairs to her consulting room at 122A Baker Street. She unlocks the door and stoops down to pick up a handful of letters. One of them, she instantly recognises, is addressed in the familiar hand of her former client Miss Rosalind Whitely.

Lucy slits open the envelope and pulls out a cheque, and a note written on fine milled notepaper.

Dear Miss Landseer (she reads)

Please find enclosed the remuneration for your investigation. I cannot begin to express my thanks for your hard work and diligence. My stepfather has now been imprisoned, awaiting trial. I regret that I cannot be sorry for him. But I am not sorry at all!

On another matter: I have decided to enrol at the Nightingale School for Nurses ~ I believe I told you that it was a profession I have always desired to enter. I am looking forward to beginning my training in a short while.

I have also taken in a lodger. Miss Amelia Ferry, whom, of course, you remember well, is coming to live with me. Her health is not good, and she needs to be looked after. She will rent out her house, and I hope, as the years progress, we will find in each other a close sorority and companionship.

Yours,

Most sincerely,

Rosalind Whitely

Lucy sets down the letter. Her first professional investigation is finished. And she solved it successfully, to her own and her client's satisfaction. She goes to the window and looks down into the street. As she stands there, idly watching the passing traffic, a carriage approaches and stops below. The coachman jumps down from the box and opens the door. A woman emerges, bonneted and heavily veiled. She glances all around, checks the address on a small card, then walks with determined step towards the house. Lucy Landseer smiles to herself. It looks as if her second professional investigation is just about to begin.

****

There are always new beginnings, but there are also endings. Euphemia Harbinger, once the cynosure of every male eye, is nearing the end of her particular journey. She knows it. Her faithful housekeeper Rose knows it, and downstairs, in the sitting room of the Chelsea house, the state of play is being discussed by her two nephews Arthur and Sherborne, who have arrived to pay their accustomed morning visit, only to be told their aunt is not receiving any visitors now or probably in the foreseeable future. Both men understand perfectly what this indicates.

"So, that is it at last. She's finally dying," Arthur Harbinger says, rubbing his hands together. "Thank God. What a long and tedious time it has been."

"But perhaps, not an unprofitable time," Sherborne remarks.

His brother regards him with an air of infinite exasperation. "Oh? Is that what you think? Well, I doubt that you are going to profit greatly from aunt's Will, little brother. After all, we both know how vilely you treated sister Wilhelmina. She has no doubt told the old fool all about it, in great detail, while she wormed her way back into her affections and stole the diamonds that should by right, have gone to me as the eldest in the family. My presumption is that a codicil will have been added cutting you out and putting her in. Now, what do you think to that?"

Sherborne's face flushes with anger. "Why should you presume it is I who have been cut out? We both know aunt took an extraordinary fancy to Harriet. I am sure she would not exclude me from her final wishes, for that reason alone. It is far more likely that she has cut YOU out ~ after all, you have no wife or family."

Arthur laughs. "You always were a fool, Sherborne. Your daughter was made a present of a book, was she not? Why should you think there is any more for her or you? No, I am sure the old woman has left the bulk of her estate to our sister ~ and it will be our job to make sure that she doesn't get her hands on it. We did it before; we will do it again."

Sherborne stares at him. "We will? How will we?"

"Nothing easier, my dear little brother. I happen to know the name of the law firm that handles aunt's affairs. Once she is dead, we will make sure there are no notices posted in any newspapers alerting our sister to the death. Then we arrange matters so that we, and only we, attend the reading of her Will. Of course, we promise the lawyer that we will write to our sister and inform her of her good fortune."

"Only we're not going to, are we?" Sherborne grins conspiratorially.

"Precisely. Now, I suggest we depart to our various establishments and await the announcement of the death. The housekeeper has been told to inform me as soon as it takes place." Arthur gestures towards the cage where the grey parrot is listening attentively, its black bead eyes shining. "Perhaps you should take that parrot back to the hotel with you."

"Wretched bird! I never wanted it in the first place. It was a birthday gift to my daughter from some friend of my wife's," Sherborne says shortly. "I'm not walking the streets carrying a cage. It can remain here. Once the old woman is dead, I shall wring its neck."

The two Harbinger brothers leave. Already, it feels as if the house is gathering around itself, preparing for the next stage in its history, its life swinging on a turning point. Once she has been reassured that they have gone, the old woman makes her way downstairs. Slowly, clinging onto the bannisters. Each step is an adventure. Every day the journey becomes more arduous. Finally, dizzy and short of breath, she arrives at the door of the sitting room. The grey parrot is bouncing excitedly up and down on its perch.

"Harriet?" it squawks upon seeing her. Then, in an exact mimicry of Sherborne Harbinger, *"Wretched bird! Once the old woman is dead, I shall wring its neck."*

Euphemia Harbinger stares hard at the bird, who continues to whistle and chirp as it sprays seed all over the Turkey rug. For some time, she stands on the threshold, holding tight to the door frame, watching the parrot. Then without a word, she makes her way to the parlour and sits down at her writing desk.

Later that afternoon, Euphemia Harbinger has a visitor. Fresh from that stronghold of melancholy, Gray's Inn, comes a pale tall man, with high shoulders and a stooping gait. It is Mr Pelham Parker, senior law clerk to Vulpis & Fox. He carries a leather document case, which, upon being shown into the parlour, he opens, extracting a pen, a legal document, and a small bottle of black ink, which he places upon the red bobbled tablecloth. He pulls up a chair and waits for the arrival of his client.

Several minutes elapse. Then he hears slow shuffling footsteps approaching. The door opens and Euphemia Harbinger enters, leaning heavily on two sticks. She is encased in shawls, despite the heat. Panting, she struggles to one of the chairs and slowly subsides into it. Her complexion reminds him of a cheese that has been left too long on the larder shelf. The senior law clerk stands and bows. She waves him back to his seat.

"Yes, yes. Let us dispense with the formalities, Mr Parker. Time is short, especially mine. I wish to change my Will once more, and that is why I have sent for you," she says, her voice thin and reedy.

He nods, respectfully. It is not the first time he has performed this action. The inclination of rich eccentric clients like Miss Harbinger to change, amend and alter their last Will and Testament is how his law firm has managed not only to survive, but prosper. The codicils to this particular document now run to five pages. He finds a fresh sheet of parchment, dips his pen into the ink and regards the blank page attentively, awaiting his instructions.

"Firstly, I desire all other bequests and codicils to be struck out. Every single one. This is my final and only Will, is that clear? This and only this. Nothing more."

He inclines his head, pen poised. She dictates. He writes. The pen moves smoothly across the paper. When she has done, she glances at him, smiling slyly. "You say nothing? Should you not be pointing out the folly of my decision? Is that not your legal duty, eh?"

The senior law clerk shrugs minutely. What the clients of Vulpis & Fox choose to do with their property, money or sundry worldly goods and chattels is entirely up to them. He merely scribes their wishes on their behalf and collects the fee.

"I shall return to chambers and draw up the new Will, which I will then dispatch for your signature. My messenger can witness it, if you wish."

"I do wish it. That sounds perfectly satisfactory. Let it be so." The old woman mumbles into silence. Her eyelids droop. Her mouth opens slightly, the lips slack. Her chest rises and falls.

The clerk gets to his feet, packs away his things and tiptoes out of the room. He goes back, on foot, to his chambers to draw up the new Will, which is signed, witnessed and returned the same day. Later, over a bottle or two of port wine at his club, he will regale his friends with the story of the rich, eccentric old lady, who left her house and contents to a ten-year old child (under the conservatorship of a senior partner of Vulpis & Fox together with her aunt), and everything else to be turned into educational bursaries for gifted girls from less well-off families.

Neither Euphemia Harbinger, nor the senior law clerk, will ever know that one of the first beneficiaries from her generosity is going to be a certain bright pupil called Violet Cully.

****

And now, once again, it is a bright Sunday morning, the sun streaming down on the city out of a cloudless blue sky. Church bells summon the faithful, the hopeful, plus those hedging their bets, to worship. A good day to live. *A good day to die*, thinks the elderly woman in the bed. She reaches out and picks up the small brass bell on her bedside table.

A couple of rings brings Rose, her faithful housekeeper, hurrying into the room, carrying a bowl of hot water, soap and a towel. The old woman waves them away. She is clean enough for the one she is about to meet. She has lain awake most of the night, listening to his footsteps approach. There is no time to subject herself to the indignities of a bed bath, her cracks and crevices subjected to the harsh flannel.

"Come here, Rose," she commands.

The housekeeper sets down the bowl and approaches the wizened stick-like figure in the bed. "Madam?"

She raises herself on her elbows. Slowly, painstakingly. Her voice is a rasped whisper.

"You know what you have to do?"

The housekeeper nods. "Shall I do it today?" she asks.

"Yes. Today. In fact, do it now," the old woman nods.

As Rose leaves the room, Euphemia Harbinger sinks back onto her pillow, a smile of wicked satisfaction on her face. Her eyes close. Her breathing becomes gradually lighter and lighter, until finally, it ceases altogether.

Meanwhile, downstairs in the sitting room, the grey parrot sidles along its perch, eying the unexpectedly open cage door. A few seconds later, it plucks up courage and moves from its gilded prison to perch on the windowsill. For a moment, the bird hesitates. Then with a soft grey flutter of wings, it takes flight, launching itself joyously out of the open window and into the freedom of an unknown future.

****

So finally, let us return briefly for one last time to a certain small upstairs room in a run-down lodging-house. It is very late at night and a candle has been lit, its flickering flame falling upon the two occupants: Little Azella, who is already tucked up in bed, and Micky Mokey, who is changing out of his clothes before going to bed himself.

"So, he's gone then?" Little Azella asks, with a yawn.

"Yes. Quite gone. I saw him leave the hotel this morning, along with his family. And he wasn't looking at all pleased, I can tell you. Face like a thunderstorm. One look at him and I knew it meant he hadn't come into the great fortune that he expected to. And that is the end of it. He has got what he deserved ~ absolutely nothing."

"And are you happy now, Micky?"

Micky Mokey smiles. "Yes, I am very happy. He has been paid back for everything he did to me, all those years ago. And he will never guess how it was done. Never in a million years. Time to go to sleep, Little Azella," he says. "Tomorrow is another day."

Micky Mokey carefully hangs up the frock coat, the bright waistcoat, the wing collared shirt, yellow paisley cravat, and the striped trousers. Finally, he unwraps the tight cotton bindings that flatten the chest, giving him the semblance of a manly physique. Then Wilhelmina Harbinger, male impersonator, blows out her candle, and climbs into bed.

Finis

Thank you for reading this book. If you have enjoyed it, why not leave a review on Amazon and recommend it to other readers? All reviews, however long or short, help me to continue doing what I do.

Printed in Great Britain
by Amazon

84524093R00129